THE FLATHEAD COUNTRY

When someone stole Ash Fitzhugh's outfit, he tracked them and caught bear-built, bearded Caleb Wolff, and his sister, Lisa. Ash intended merely to retrieve his property and then move on, but unexpected gunshots soon changed his mind. From that point on, his life turned into a puzzle between what was right and what was wrong. He finally joined the man the Wolffs despised — and that was when the trouble really began . . .

CONCHO BRADLEY

THE FLATHEAD COUNTRY

Complete and Unabridged

LINFORD
Leicester

First published in Great Britain in 1996 by
Robert Hale Limited
London

First Linford Edition
published 1997
by arrangement with
Robert Hale Limited
London

British Library CIP Data

Bradley, Concho, *1916* –
    The flathead country.—Large print ed.—
Linford western library
    1. Western stories
    2. Large type books
    I. Title
    813.5'4 [F]

    ISBN 0–7089–5144–9

Published by
F. A. Thorpe (Publishing) Ltd.
Anstey, Leicestershire

Set by Words & Graphics Ltd.
Anstey, Leicestershire
Printed and bound in Great Britain by
T. J. International Ltd., Padstow, Cornwall

This book is printed on acid-free paper

1

Introduction to a New Country

WHEN Ash Fitzhugh reached the Snake River country he did not know, exactly, where he was, but the land was a stockman's paradise.

Aside from the river there were creeks, small lakes, miles of flat to rolling graze, timber within reach, and because he arrived there in late spring the days were warm and long, the nights were cold, and game was abundant.

He thought he was in Montana, the nearly unreadable map he had used to find this country had been drawn by a bearded bear of a man he had met in New Mexico, who swore he had been over every mile of it, and he probably had, but not in Idaho, in Montana.

It did not really matter. What he wanted was livestock country, graze, water, timber for buildings and privacy. He satisfied himself about the privacy after saddlebacking over dozens of miles and only turned back when he could distantly make out mountains to the north and east and a lava bed where the grazing country ended south of the mountains.

It was a good thirty mile ride to get back where he had set up camp and since it was not possible to get back there in one day, most of which he had spent exploring, he hobbled his horse in stirrup-high grass, bedded down near a clearwater creek and would have had an uninterrupted sleep except for two cub bears about the size of dogs which came to forage, and whose short, grunting sounds woke him.

Where there were cub bears there was also a sow bear. The moon lacked half of being full but visibility was good enough for Ash to pull on his boots, take a stick and chase the cubs away. In their flight they made frightened little whining yelps.

Ash went back and sat with his saddlegun across his lap until predawn but the sow bear did not appear.

He struck out during false dawn, rode all day except for periods of rest for his horse, and reached his camp with the moon rising.

His food cache had been emptied and the entire camp ransacked. Except for his beltgun and carbine, the clothes he was standing in, and odds and ends which had been flung aside, Ash Fitzhugh had been thoroughly raided, and obviously, since what had been stolen had been carried away, it had not been varmints.

Of his three blankets the only one he still had was the same one rolled behind his cantle which he had used the night the cubs came visiting.

Animals, bears, cougars, wolves, might shred blankets but they would not carry them away. Nor would they carry away a cache of food, they would eat or destroy it where they had found it.

He made a little fire, wrapped his remaining blanket around his shoulders and kept warm until morning. If he slept he had no recollection of it.

Ash had learned to read sign during childhood when he'd hunted rabbits, but even if he hadn't known how, he could have tracked the raiders because they made no effort to conceal their trail. Not at first anyway.

That he was not the only two-legged creature in the area did not surprise him. But he had seen no rising smoke, no worn pathways, no burnt stone rings.

When he came to a creek he knew what to expect, the raiders would go up or down the water course until they decided to leave it, the idea being that a tracker would lose them. But these raiders did not bother, they slogged across the creek and emerged on the far side leaving wet tracks a blind man could have followed.

Ash formed opinions as he tracked,

there had been two raiders. From the depth of their tracks one was heavier than the other. The heavier one was the leader. By the time the sun was directly overhead Ash had reached rising country with trees. He halted beside a little waterway, saw trout minnows scatter when his shadow fell upon the water and sat on a large rock. Here, the tracks showed very plainly in creek-side moist earth. The lead raider had larger feet than his companion.

Some time later he caught a faint scent of smoke. Not having come down in the last rain he sought a high place to scan the area, but there were too many trees for more than a spotty view. He did not see the source of the smoke scent, just a vast amount of rugged country.

When he resumed tracking the imprints began edging westerly. There was no chance that the raid on his camp had been a random affair, a matter of accidental discovery, and that meant his pursuit had probably not gone unobserved.

He considered continuing afoot. The reason he didn't was because the raiders understandably would be watching their back trail. If he tied the horse and went ahead on foot, whatever he found, when he got back the horse would not be there.

He had not kept track of time, so when shadows began to form on his off side, he paused just long enough to seek the sun past treetops and thought it had to be about mid-afternoon when he abruptly emerged from the trees on a ridge, overlooking a long, narrow valley with a large log house at its northernmost end — lazy tendrils of wood smoke rising from a stove pipe.

The tracks did not go north in the direction of the house, they went south as though to utilize all cover to avoid detection and that was a disappointment.

He followed the tracks with the sun steadily declining, reconciled that he would have to spend another night with his only blanket in whatever shelter he came across.

It occurred to him as he tracked that whoever the raiders were, they just might be leading him all over the country on purpose, and if this were so, probably with day fading, they would be atop some point of vantage watching him.

He was convinced what he would eventually find was the same kind of poverty, hostility and gauntness he had seen in the aftermath of the Civil War where a thoroughly defeated Confederacy had been left whipped, starved and demoralized. Except that this was — he still believed he was in Montana — about as far as a man could get from the south without being in a foreign country.

He tracked right up until an early dusk, then sought, and found, a suitable place to bed down. He hobbled the horse in a postage-stamp-sized clearing, ate jerky, tanked up on creek water, lighted a tiny fire to keep warm by and with the blanket around his shoulders, sat down to rest.

Later, in a moonless night as dark as the inside of a boot, he used his saddle blanket to fill out the blanket roll, left his hat beside his bedroll and faced south-westerly where brush and tree cover was more than adequate.

If he was guessing wrong this would be his second night with little or no sleep. He dryly told himself this wouldn't be the first time he'd missed out on sleep and likely wouldn't be the last time.

He watched the grazing horse more than taking the pulse of the surrounding area. A horse could be depended upon to scent anything unexpected by daylight or dark. Ash Fitzhugh's horse was no exception.

The cold steadily increased as the night wore along. There were the inevitable night-foraging intruders. A brace of raccoons attracted by a strange scent, and four wormy coyotes whose winter hair clung in patches, and a mouse-hunting owl who swooped low on silent wings, saw the man and furiously beat his way higher where he disappeared in darkness.

It was a long wait, a very long wait in fact; they didn't arrive until the night was at the coldest, just ahead of false dawn.

The bay horse, which had been hip-shot dozing, gradually raised its head, little ears pointing. Ash estimated that they were coming from the west and slightly southward, were approaching behind him. The possibility existed that they had watched him make the little fire and punch up the blanket to look like a sleeping man, and if this were the case his ambush might work in reverse.

Alternately he watched the horse and strained for sounds. The horse was more reliable; whoever they were, probably from practice, they knew how to move soundlessly.

Only once did he pick up sound and that was when someone not too distant behind him inadvertently stepped on loose rocks and they rattled.

He wanted to face around but didn't; movement would be discernible.

By the time he thought they were close enough to his hiding place they moved northward. The horse followed this altered course by turning, little ears pointing.

They stopped near the foremost stand of trees bordering the little meadow. Ash moved only his head. When he saw them they were sashaying back and forth like coursing Indians.

He eased low an inch at a time, pushed his saddlegun ahead and waited for additional movement. But there was none, instead there was a ghost-like almost inaudible sound of loud whispering.

" . . . Just the horse. You set beside the bedroll. If he wakes up shove your gun barrel in his ear."

Ash saw one wraith come into the clearing. Weak starshine reflected off a six-gun the raider had in his right hand. In his left hand he had a short lariat.

The second wraith appeared heading for his camp. This one was smaller. Both wore coats, hats, and other attire dark enough to be unnoticed until they moved.

Ash settled forward with the Winchester in both hands. Each time the tall one approached the horse it sidled away. Ash watched, understood the tall raider's frustration, he'd had the same trouble with the bay horse for years. The purpose of hobbles was to make it easy to catch horses. Some horses developed an ability to rabbit-hop with hobbles faster than a man could run.

Ash devised a way to prevent this long ago, but the tall man trying to reach the horse was being teased as the animal hopped just out of reach.

The man swore fiercely through his teeth. He stood stone still watching the bay horse. It did the same, it watched the man in dark clothing.

The short raider got as far as the

opposite side of the dying little fire and squatted. Because this one had its back to Ash he could not see the bedroll or even the dying little fire.

His intention was to wait until the tall one knelt to remove the hobbles. He did not worry much about the one with his back to his place of concealment.

But it began to appear the horse was not going to be caught. In fact the longer the tall raider tried to get close enough to get a rope on the bay, the more it kept distance between itself and the man.

The tall one turned abruptly and hissed. His companion arose, abandoned his role as watcher and started to hike toward the tall one.

Another time Ash would have been amused. He settled lower, watched the small raider go out where his companion spoke through gritted teeth. "I'd like to kill that son of a bitch. See what you can do." As the shorter raider took the rope the horse dropped its head to crop grass, and Ash smiled to himself. His horse did not stop watching the dark wraiths. This was part of a game he played; he would act unconcerned right up until the short raider got close, then do his sidling trick.

The short raider had no better luck than his companion had had, but in that one's favour, there was a demonstration of patience.

Ash watched, knew how the raiders felt, and when they left the horse to approach Ash's camp, he allowed them to get within a few feet of it before cocking the Winchester.

Both raiders froze. He let them sweat for a long moment before telling them to drop their pistols. They obeyed without hesitation. He then ordered them to lock their fingers atop their heads and after this had been done Ash shrugged out of his dirt and leaf cover, walked close with the cocked Winchester in both hands, and told them to shed their hats. Again he was obeyed without hesitation — and got a shock. The short raider's hair tumbled over both shoulders.

He moved a little closer, staring, before he said, "What's your name?"

The girl did not answer, the man did. "Leave her out of it. My name's Caleb Wolff — with two f's."

Ash eased off the saddlegun's hammer, let the gun sag and, acting as though he had not heard the tall one he said, "For the last time, what's your name!"

This time he got a quick answer. "Lisa Wolff with two f's."

Ash returned his attention to the man. "Where do you live?"

"A mile or so south of here on a piney wood bluff."

"Get a good view from the bluff, do you?"

Caleb nodded without speaking. It required no mental giant to understand what had been behind their captor's question.

"Where's my gatherings you stole?"

"They're safe."

"Caleb, you're beginnin' to annoy me. Who is at your home place?"

"My pa."

"All right, you two come with me while I get the horse then you can lead the way to your camp."

Caleb walked ahead. "You can't catch that damned horse."

Ash said nothing. When they were in the centre of the little meadow Ash told his prisoners to sit down and not to move, then he caught the horse the only way it could be done. Ash approached slightly to one side. The horse promptly sidled in the opposite direction. Ash went in that direction. This time when the horse was preparing to hop Ash got directly in front of him. The horse dropped its head to be caught.

When Ash led the horse back he said, "You got to play checkers, he moves one way, you block that an' he'll move in the other direction, then you get right up close in front an' he quits. Isn't really a good checkers player but

15

we been partners a long time. Get up; walk back to the camp so's I can rig out for the hike to your pa's place . . . Caleb, if you got a belly gun an' fish for it while we're walkin' the second you start to turn I'll blow your head off."

It was as cold as the proverbial witch's bosom. Daylight was coming but that was no consolation, the sun would provide no heat for an hour after the sun arrived.

Ash rode a couple of yards behind his prisoners. Neither of them spoke nor moved to look back.

Ash's first view of the Wolff place was with golden sunlight over his shoulder. The setting was ideal, a large meadow, shade trees, a squatly log barn and a log house with geraniums growing along the front where three broad steps led to a porch.

There were signs of poor care or no care. There was a slab-sided, floppy-eared dog who stood in front of the

16

house wagging its tail without making a sound.

Smoke was rising above a crooked stove pipe, and as Ash herded his captives toward the house the door flung violently open and an elderly man who badly needed shearing appeared on the porch holding a long barrelled hunting rifle. He had an old hawgleg six-shooter in a holster on the right side of a battered old shellbelt.

Where the pair of raiders halted Ash raised the six-gun from his lap and quietly addressed the old man with the mop of unkempt grey hair. "Mister Wolff, put the gun down." When the old man did not move Ash leaned, cocked his Colt and aimed it at the back of Caleb's head. He only had to hold that position moments before the old man stepped to the porch railing and leaned his weapon there. As he straightened up he glared. "Who are you, an' what you think you're doin' drivin' Cal an' Lisa ahead of you! If you ride for that son of a bitch — "

"Pa!" the girl exclaimed. "He's not one of 'em. He's the stranger Cal an' me brought all that stuff from. The one we saw smoke risin' over a camp down below. His name's — " The girl stopped and turned.

"Ash Fitzhugh, Mister Wolff."

She repeated it. "Ash Fitzhugh, Pa."

"An' how come him to be herdin' you like sheep, Lisa?"

The answer came reluctantly. "We went after his horse. He out-foxed us."

"You two was goin' to be horse thieves, Lisa!"

"Pa, we got to have a horse."

The old man stood stiffly, hostility in every line of his face. "Put your horse in the barn," he said to Ash, and turned on his daughter. "That's where you was come sun-up . . . Caleb . . . we'll talk about this later. Lisa, fire up the stove. Caleb, wait for Mister Fitzhugh an' fetch him to the house. Horse thieves! What'n tarnation is this family comin' to!"

2

The Wolff Clan

THE barn smelled musty. Since there was a loft ladder he guessed hay had been stored up there a long time. He crawled up to see if it was fit to feed a horse and got another surprise. There was a whiskey still up there complete with copper coils and a small cooker. It hadn't been the scent of mouldy hay that had attracted Ash's attention, but there was hay down below in an open stall, fresh cut with the scythe leaning nearby.

He fed the bay and headed for the house. Without any warning someone in the northerly wood lot fired a carbine. The bullet threw up a gout of dirt several feet on Ash's left side.

Before Ash could act, someone at

the house fired back with a rifle, not a carbine. Ash reached the porch swiftly and with Colt in hand shoved his way inside. The old man was leaning his rifle aside. His daughter was in the kitchen. Caleb told Ash calmly he could put up his pistol, and Lisa called from the kitchen that dinner was ready.

Ash looked from the old man to his son. Caleb said, "He fires one round, we fire back an' he don't come back until tomorrow."

Lisa smiled at Ash as she pointed to a chair. He watched the old man and his son dive into their meal. When he looked up Lisa was regarding him from over by the stove. There was a twinkle of dry amusement in her gaze. "Eat," she said.

Ash answered curtly, "He came within an ace of shootin' me."

The old man raised a shaggy head with small, faded blue eyes and spoke around a mouthful of food. "He don't try to kill."

"Who is he?" Ash asked.

"We got no idea which one he is. Nolan's got three hired riders. It's one of them or Nolan himself."

"How long's this been goin' on?"

"Since last spring," the old man replied, reaching for his coffee cup. "Mister Fitzhugh, you got to understand we aren't leavin'. As for the shootin', when we work out how to pay him back, we'll do it. Eat your supper, Mister Fitzhugh."

The springtime evening daylight lingered. The old man, who had been sitting on the porch for years, had decided some months back to do his resting in the barn, which is what he did after supper. Lisa stayed behind. Caleb, a rugged, taciturn man followed his father and Ash Fitzhugh brought up the rear.

Down there, with that aroma Ash had mistaken for spoiling hay, the old man sat on a rickety stool, Caleb sat on a small wooden keg and jutted his jaw for Ash to sit on another small wooden keg.

Caleb got a cud of molasses cured tucked into his cheek and his father repeated what he'd been saying since Caleb took up chewing. "If your ma was alive she wouldn't let you in the house doin' that."

Caleb settled his back against the log wall and gazed steadily ahead. His mother had been dead since Lisa had come along; Caleb had been five. He acted as though his father had not spoken.

The old man shoved out a thick, calloused hand. "Name's Willford, Mister Fitzhugh. Folks been callin' me Will since I was a button."

Ash gripped the hand and settled back as the old man said, "You'll get your gatherings back. I never minded 'em raidin' a little but I didn't raise horsethieves." The old man paused. "Where you from Mister Fitzhugh?"

"I was born in Alabama but worked cattle in Texas an' New Mexico. I figured I'd earned some time off so I come to Montana."

Both Will and Caleb Wolff stared in long silence. Eventually Caleb said, "You're in Idaho, not Montana. To get up there you got to ride north a month or so."

Ash was shocked but not upset. As he was absorbing this information, Will Wolff asked another question. "You lookin' for ranch work?"

"No, not until I run out of money."

Caleb made another dry announcement. "If you was lookin' for a place to start up, Mister Fitzhugh, this isn't the country. We had some notion of makin' a go with cattle." Caleb paused to expectorate. "Only feller in this country who runs cattle is Fred Nolan. If you try to buck him, somethin' will happen to your cattle, an' after that if he can't buy out pennies on the dollar, he does other things."

Ash considered Caleb's strong, saturnine profile. "Like shootin' at you in your own yard?"

Caleb nodded without speaking.

Ash faced the old man. "Where's the

23

law, a sheriff or a constable?"

"Not within four days' ride, an' they don't take sides against stockmen." As the old man finished speaking he hunched forward with both chapped, calloused hands between his knees. "Go somewhere else, Mister Fitzhugh, an' start up your cattle outfit. I've heard that over in Wyoming it's possible for a man to get started with beef, but not with sheep. They've had shootin' wars over there when sheep come along."

Ash hadn't said he wanted to start up in the cattle trade, although for the past few years he'd thought about it. In fact when he scouted up the country from his first camp, the idea had grown stronger in his mind.

"Mister Wolff, who is Fred Nolan? I mean, where's his outfit an' — "

"You wouldn't like workin' for him," the old man interrupted to say. "He don't hire 'em on unless they're meaner'n a snake an' hard enough to chew nails an' spit rust."

"I wasn't thinkin' of hirin' on with

him," Ash stated. "I was curious, is all. He's been a year tryin' to run you off. Has he done this to anyone else?"

Again Caleb answered without looking around; his tone was as craggy as it had been before. "He's burnt 'em out, scairt 'em out, an', so they say, tried to buy 'em out like he done with us, for pennies on the dollar."

Ash shifted on the keg, resettled his shoulders against the logs at his back and did not move until Will Wolff groaned up to his feet as he said, "Cal an' Lisa'll get your gatherings. You can pack 'em out with you in the morning."

Ash made no move to arise, he looked up at the old man. "How long'll you put up with Nolan?"

Will sat down again. "Until we can figure things. There's only me'n Caleb. He's got three riders an' the son of a bitch himself. He's a moneyed man, runs hundreds of cattle, don't own all the land he runs over but he don't tolerate anyone tryin' to get set up

25

on land he's used for years. Mister Fitzhugh, I'm not a bushwhackin' man, wasn't raised to be one an' didn't raise Cal to be one, but Gawd's my witness I been tempted these last couple of years. We started up a nice little herd, good up-graded animals. It disappeared. Rustled for a fact but it rained for a week afterwards so there was no tracks to follow."

Caleb abruptly came out of his reverie and stood up. "Pa, Mister Fitzhugh don't want to know all this." Caleb looked at Ash. "We'll put your gatherings in the barn in the mornin'."

For a moment Ash thought the taciturn man was going to apologize for raiding him. Instead Caleb left the barn in the direction of the house without adding anything to what he had said. His father hung back watching his son, and sighed. "He's proud, Mister Fitzhugh. When his mother died he was a long time comin' to grips with it. Now, he's sort of crawled into himself. He's a good lad. He thought we should pull stakes an' find another place. Maybe over in Wyoming . . . Mister Fitzhugh, my wife's buried here. She was my life. I'd never set easy knowin' there'd be no one to keep wolves an' coyotes from diggin' in her grave. I told Caleb to go, get on his own. That's what makes it so hard for him'n me to talk. Sometimes I wish he'd go. But I'd miss him . . . Let's go over to the house and settle. I make good whiskey."

Ash went as far as the long steps to the porch before stopping. "How do cattle disappear?" he asked, and got a slightly caustic sidelong look along with his answer. "When Fred Nolan makes 'em disappear."

They went inside. Lisa was no longer dressed in black. She had looped two braids and fixed them in place with an intricate bow of red ribbon. Her face shone by lamplight. She didn't smile at Ash but offered him coffee and motioned toward a chair.

Her father said, "Whiskey, Lisa. Coffee's all right, but — "

She looked steadily at the old man when she interrupted him. "We hike thirty miles for supplies. Mash'n whatnot to make whiskey in the loft. We could pack flour'n sugar in the place we use for whiskey makin'."

The old man sank into a chair smiling. "If I had wings I could do it round-trip in half, maybe a third of the time."

She made a disgusted grunt and went to the kitchen. When she returned with the bottle and two cups, the old man said, "You're pretty as a spotted bird. Don't go around with your mouth pulled down." He was pouring when he also said, "We come through a lot the three of us. We'll come through a lot more. Hand this cup to Mister Fitzhugh. Thank you . . . Lisa, I'd take it kindly if you'd put Mister Fitzhugh's gatherings in the barn in the mornin'."

"The sugar too?" she said.

Ash spoke up. "Keep the sugar."

She glanced at him. "It's not like we like takin' handouts, but there's some things, when we run out, it's awful hard to get by without."

Ash nodded agreeably. "Where's the nearest town an' store?"

"Sixty miles," old Will replied. "Through mountainous country. The town is called Wildroot."

Ash sipped whiskey until he began feeling warm all over then put the cup aside. "You got a horse, Mister Wolff?"

"Not any more. We had four, two harness an' two for saddle. They died one at a time over a period of about five or six months."

"How do you haul supplies?"

"On our backs, Mister Fitzhugh, an' I know what you're thinkin' but like I said in the barn, I'll give up the ghost right here in the yard before I'll let that son of a bitch run us off."

Ash considered the whiskey in his cup and raised his eyes to find Lisa regarding him solemnly. He drained the cup, shot up to his feet and said he would bunk down in the loft. At the doorway the old man said, "They had a reason for tryin' to steal your horse, but there's nothin' on this earth lower'n a horse thief. I didn't raise 'em to do that. In the mornin' I'll see to it that they apologize."

Ash smiled and crossed the yard under a scimitar moon to the barn. Sleeping in a loft where there was a working still was not an altogether unpleasant experience, in fact when he awakened in the morning just ahead of sunrise he felt fifteen years younger than his thirty-four years.

His horse had been fed and the Wolffs were piling what they had raided from his camp. He heard them talking. When the old man said, "We'll go directly, Lisa. I know how you feel an' I got to tell you, you'n Caleb been real troopers. We'll go for supplies in the next few days an' we'll pack back nothin' for the still."

Ash waited until they left the barn before climbing down. He went out back to the trough to clean up. When he appeared over at the house he was made welcome. Breakfast was both plentiful and tasteful. He told Lisa he'd never eat better anywhere, and she blushed.

Hauling back all that had been stolen from him required two croaker sacks and his blanket tied at both ends to make a tube.

He didn't go back the way he had reached the Wolff place, Caleb showed him a worn trail which angled down from the bluff. In fact he could see where his camp had been before he'd used this trail for a hundred yards.

It also cut hours off the ride. The sun was still high when he unloaded, hobbled his horse to graze and set about arranging things the way they had been before the raid.

He boiled jerky in creek water, finished supper about sundown and sat by the little cooking fire for a long time before rolling into his blankets.

He explored for two days, until he began to find his own tracks, then yielded to an urge to ride up the snake-like trail to the Wolff place.

He got up there with the sun directly above. The old dog came out to greet him. He dismounted, put his horse in the barn and followed the dog to the house. The door was padlocked. The dog stood at his side looking up. Ash went to a porch chair and sat down. The dog sprawled beside the chair. He scratched it as he said, "How long ago did they leave?"

The dog rolled on to its back, forepaws held wide. He scratched its stomach.

The dog was asleep and did not move when Ash left the porch, returned to the barn, studied the ground until he knew which way the Wolffs had gone, then went back to rig out the bay and follow tracks made by three people, two with large feet, one with small feet. There was a trail, evidently used by the old man and his son and daughter. It was easy to follow because the tracks did not leave the trail.

But he could not make good time, there were few places flat enough to lope, but where it was possible and not hard on the bay, he trotted.

If the Wolffs had left a day or two earlier he did not expect to meet them unless it was on their return trip. If they had left later, possibly the day he had ridden to the bluff, it was possible he could overtake them.

He had to yield to prudence in some places as the sun sank. There were sheer drop-offs on both sides of bony ridges good enough for two-legged things but dangerous for a mounted man.

He got a fair idea of the country as he rode, and except for a few meadows, or spongy places where water ran, it was mountainous with timbered places. At best it was marginal livestock country.

He called it quits when he found a

likely small clearing. With dusk coming the trail was too risky. He hobbled the hungry animal, unrolled his blanket from aft of the cantle, walked to a creek to wash and gather twigs. He had nothing to cook nor anything to cook it in, but jerky, the rangeman's companion, could be eaten straight from the pocket. The African Moors who conquered Spain and ruled it for 700 years had lived on it — they called it *jarqui*.

His original objective had been to overtake the Wolffs and offer his horse to help pack supplies, but when he rolled out the second morning with a fairly good view of the onward countryside he saddled up while thinking they must have left their home place a day earlier than he had thought.

He smiled while mounting and reining over to the trail. The girl's outburst to her father had made it clear that while she would pack her share of supplies, she resented having to pack what she considered superfluous baggage with which to supply the old man's still.

Well, women were not great whiskey drinkers, particularly inexperienced, young ones.

The bay horse abruptly changed leads. It was hiking along with its head raised staring toward a neighbouring ridge. Ash only caught a glimpse of movement. He told the bay it could have been a rutting buck, a big cat or maybe a bear, but whatever it was the sight of a rider had spooked it.

Warmth eventually arrived. The day was cloudless with perfect visibility. As far as Ash could see to the east and north was inhospitable, broken country with tier after tier of serrated rims. No one in his right mind would try to run livestock in that kind of country, which occasioned an interesting speculation; if someone named Nolan successfully ranched this area it had to be south and west — unless up ahead where the town was, there was grazing country. But as he slouched along pondering, that didn't make much sense; if the Nolan outfit was in the area of the Wolff place, then the land south and west had to be better than what he had been riding through since the day before.

He had never before been so abruptly startled as he was the moment someone fired a gun on ahead and westerly. Even the bay horse, who had been dozing along, slammed to a stiff-legged halt, head up, little ears pointing in the direction of the echo.

For Ash, the prudent thing was to leave the trail, get lost in the tangled westward region. As he reined in that direction he told himself it had been a hunter. He had seen plentiful game tracks since first arriving in what he had thought was Montana.

The second gunshot was louder, clearly made by a pistol. After a moment the person who had fired first, fired again, clearly using either a rifle or a carbine, the sounds were very different.

36

Ash followed a game trail down a slope into a long, narrow place of trees, grass and underbrush, all fed by a busy little cold-water creek.

He tied the bay among trees, which provided a good hiding place, took his Winchester and followed the creek on its erratic north-westerly route.

He did not find the gunman, he did better, he found a tethered grey horse branded FN on the left shoulder.

There were some weathered large rocks on the lee side of the creek. He went in among them, sat down and got comfortable. He had the grey horse in sight.

There was no more gunfire, time passed, the sun shifted, frail shadows appeared in the arroyo and someone coming from the north scuffed stones.

Ash had leaned the Winchester aside. He followed the sound of footsteps with his six-gun resting atop a rock in his right hand.

When the man appeared he went to the horse, shoved a carbine into a saddle boot and paused to build and light a smoke. He was not young, nor was he old. There was grey around his ears. He was a lanky individual who wore his belt gun low and tied to his leg. Ash had known his share of rangemen. He pegged this one as trouble four ways from the middle, so when the stranger had lighted his quirly Ash cocked the six-gun. The stranger did not move, did not in fact even seem to be breathing.

The grey horse too had been unprepared for the ominous snippet of sound and faced toward the boulders.

The lean man harshly said, "Spit or close the window!"

Ash arose from among the rocks. "Drop it!" he said.

The stranger emptied his holster and slowly turned his head. They looked steadily at each other for a long moment before the stranger with a slit for a mouth said, "I know who you are. Take some good advice, mister. Get on your horse an' don' even look back."

Ash nodded. "Who was you shootin' at?"

"None of your damned business. Get on your horse an' — "

Ash had a question. "You work for a feller named Nolan?"

"That's none of your damned business neither."

"If you don't, mister, an' you're ridin' a horse wearin' his brand, you're a horse thief. Where I come from we hang 'em on sight."

The lean man's face was weathered to the colour of old leather, his pale eyes were close-spaced and venomous. When next he spoke it was to reiterate what he'd said earlier, and add more to it. "Mister, we seen you ridin' around down by the lava beds. We seen you at the Wolff place. We don't know nothin' about you an' don' want to know, but if you're stickin' your nose where it don't belong, let me tell you — you'll get buried up here."

Ash's reply was curt. "Untie your horse, dump that saddlegun an' lead the horse south along the creek until I tell you to stop. *Move, you son of a bitch!*"

The lean man moved. He had no difficulty about untying and leading the grey horse but he was clearly reluctant to drop the Winchester and leave it behind as he walked southward.

When they reached the place where Ash's bay was waiting, Ash used the rangeman's lariat to drop the noose over the lean man's head, snug it up around his gullet, and step clear as he said, "Get astride. If you want a broken neck run for it. I got two dallies. If you got a belly gun an' so much as move your hands where I can't see 'em I'll kill you. Start riding."

"Which way?"

"Toward the Wolff place, and keep your damned mouth shut!"

3

Out of the Night!

IT was a long ride; what made it so was the fact that Ash had to select pathways suitable to one man steering the other.

Only once did the lipless, snake-eyed man speak, and that was when Ash told him to mind a steep down grade. The man said, "What do you figure to accomplish by this?"

Ash flicked the rope to remind the rangeman he still had dallies and did not answer.

It was dusk before Ash thought about camping overnight. Thought about it but didn't do it. They were on the trail made by the Wolffs, the same trail Ash had used going north. There was adequate starlight and moonlight for the horses to slog along a well-marked trail.

41

It was cold and dawn before Ash was in familiar territory. He could make out the Wolff log house. His prisoner rode as though he had a ramrod up his back. When eventually they halted at the Wolff barn where Ash jerked his head for his prisoner to dismount, the man swung to the ground and in his almost detached, mean tone of voice said Ash had made the biggest mistake of his life, to which Ash said, "You'll be part of it. What's your name?"

The mean-faced man replied without hesitation "Bill Jones."

Ash smiled without humour and jerked his head. "Go over to the porch, Mister Jones," and aided the other man's stride by punching him over the kidneys with a gun barrel.

The morning was beginning to show warmth as they sat in chairs on old man Wolff's porch. Bill Jones rolled and lighted a smoke. He offered makings to his captor and got a negative wag of the head. Jones dryly said, "Beats hell out of deep breathin' when you're hungry."

Ash asked who Jones had been shooting at and got the same indifferent reply he'd gotten when he'd asked the question before. "Trespassers. Folks don't like trespassers; do you?"

"Who is 'folks'?"

Jones deeply inhaled and exhaled looking dead ahead across the yard. When it became evident he was not going to answer, Ash unwound up out of his chair, reached for a handful of cloth and yanked Jones to his feet. He said, "For the last time — who is 'folks'?"

"Fred Nolan."

Ash punched Jones back down on to his chair but remained leaning against the porch railing as he regarded the other man. "It was the Wolffs you was shootin' at. If you horse me around again I'll stomp the waddin' out of you."

Jones woodenly inclined his head. "Trespassers."

"You do the shootin' into this yard every day or two?"

43

Jones's gaze smouldered. "Mister, you're buttin' in where you could get bad hurt."

"Yeah, you told me that before. Is that you that shoots into the yard?"

Jones's smouldering gaze never wavered. "I answered all the questions I expect to answer," he said, and arose in order not to be surprised and yanked up right again.

Ash leaned off the railing and Jones said, "Shed the six-gun an' I'll break you to lead."

Ash jerked his head sideways for Jones to go down off the porch into the yard, which Jones did, and turned wearing a menacing smile. He told Ash this was his second mistake, and rushed, head down, arms wide with fingers bent like talons.

The surprise was not unexpected. Ash sidestepped and swung low as Jones went past, the blow brought him to a faltering halt, but it hadn't been hard enough to hurt him.

When he came around he snarled,

"One of them dance-hall fighters are you?" and began a solid, flat-footed advance, again wearing a menacing grin.

Ash moved right, forcing Jones to change lead and briefly stand with one foot off the ground. When Jones turned, Ash moved to the left. Again Jones shifted but this time Ash hit him once on the side of the head, and the next time over the heart.

Jones stopped, arm half raised, fists still balled as he regarded the man who had just hurt him. He suddenly dropped his arms and said, "This ain't settlin' anythin'," and would have said more but Ash moved like a striking snake and the sound of bone over bone was loud enough to be heard at the barn, and Bill Jones collapsed without a sound.

Ash went out back to the trough to clean up and soak sore hands in cold water. When he returned to the wide doorless front opening of the barn, three people bearing huge packs were leaning over Mister Jones.

Ash left the barn, got close so he would not have to raise his voice and said, "That's Bill Jones. He rides for Nolan. He's the feller who shot at you on the trail."

He explained how he had happened to be on the Wolffs' mesa, and how he had followed sign along the northward trail.

Caleb spat amber and shook his head in the Nolan-rider's direction. "I'll tell you somethin', Mister Fitzhugh, this is the same man who's been shootin' into the yard."

"How do you know that?"

"Because of the pattern he fired at us on the trail back, it's the same pattern he uses when he shoots into the yard."

Jones groaned, blinked, rolled over and got unsteadily to his feet. He looked at the people surrounding him, and settled his cold, menacing gaze on Ash, who asked Jones the same question he'd asked before. "You shoot into the yard every day or so? Mister Jones, next time I'll break your neck."

Jones grumbled his reply. "Sometimes it's me, other times it's someone else."

Caleb growled at Jones. "How much does Nolan pay you?"

"Twenty a month an' keep." Jones considered Caleb. He had seen him many times before and only one thing interested him: Caleb Wolff would walk some miles into the badlands and spend entire afternoons practising with his six-gun.

Jones shifted his gaze to the old man. "You're real hard to convince. Mister Nolan's young compared to you. He can wait you out."

The old man had a bitter and ready reply. "He's goin' to have to sprout an eye between his shoulders."

Ash took Jones to the barn, watched him saddle up and lead the horse out front before mounting. He sat a moment looking down before he said, "That carbine cost me nine dollars."

"You know where it is, go get it.

47

Mister Jones, one more shot into the yard an' take my word for it, you'll regret it."

Ash jerked his head. They all watched the mean-faced rangeman ride northward, continued to watch until he was out of sight, then Caleb growled as he headed for the house to get rid of a heavy pack.

Ash trailed along. At the porch the old man faced him. "I expect we owe you, but to tell you the truth, I'm not sure you been helpful."

Ash closed the front door after himself, watched Lisa, the old man and Caleb sort out their supplies. There were two sugar sacks in Lisa's pack. She caught him watching her and ignored his gaze as she and Caleb carried most of the supplies to the kitchen.

The old man went in there too, but returned shortly with two cups and an earthenware jug. As he handed Ash a cup he said, "I'm gettin' a mite long in the tooth for this back-packin' business."

He filled both cups, went to stand with his back to Ash at the small front-wall window and sipped. By the time he felt human again Lisa and Caleb had finished in the kitchen and came to the parlour. Until then he did not add more to what he had told Ash, now, showing little evidence of being tired, he said, "Caleb, what we talked about often enough an' never done, got done for us today. Nolan'll lash back."

The taciturn, bearded younger man's reply was, "It's about time, Pa. Mister Fitzhugh got it goin'."

Caleb looked at Ash. "You rode up here to visit?"

"Yes, to see how things were goin'. I wasn't surprised that you folks wasn't here. I rode over your trail and was about to turn back because I couldn't find you, when that gunfight started. I figured about where Nolan's man would be, ambushed him and brought him back."

The old man nodded toward Ash's

49

untouched cup. "I only make sippin' whiskey."

Ash obligingly sipped and the old man was right; he didn't make rotgut nor popskull, his whiskey was indeed made for enjoyment.

When Ash put the cup aside he said, "You folks know the best way to handle trouble? Don't wait for it to come to you, or you'll be defendin' yourselves. Hit the other feller first and as hard as you can. That way he's on the defensive."

At the blank looks he got after that statement, Ash clinched his own position as part of the Wolff opposition by saying, "He's goin' to take what happened to his bushwhacker hard. He'll strike back. If we're holed up here he's got to come here to do it. Tonight? Tomorrow? Caleb you know the way he'll come to get here from his home place?"

"Yes."

"Suppose me'n you take along somethin' to eat, and as soon as

50

it's dark enough, we go set up a bushwhack?"

Lisa, bothered by this abrupt turn from tolerating harassment to aggressive resistance, was faintly scowling when she told them the odds were too great. Her father, committed and willing, replied that the longer they put off fighting back the less chance they would have to do so. His meaning was clear to Lisa; they had a willing stranger.

Lisa went to the kitchen to prepare supper. The men went out to the porch to discuss details. The old man thought he should accompany Ash and Caleb. His son growled about that. "An' who'll be here to mind Lisa if it comes to that?"

It was a silent supper among preoccupied people. When it was over Lisa handed her brother and Ash Fitzhugh two small bundles. She and her father watched them leave the yard. They were invisible before they reached timber, although the moon's

51

glow was steadily increasing.

One thing Ash was learning; Montana or Idaho, as soon as the sun departed it got cold. He might discover if he lived long enough that this was as true in midsummer as it was in winter.

Caleb was a seasoned walker, his stride was wide and thrusting. Ash followed through places the only thing he could see clearly was his companion's back.

Where Caleb finally halted and leaned on his Winchester there was a broad trail between two randomly piled prehistoric dark lava rocks. Caleb glanced enquiringly and Ash nodded his head.

After they got settled, blended perfectly with the rocks and the timber-blocked moon, Caleb said, "You got a reason to expect they'll strike back the same day you roughed up their rider?"

"Just a guess," Ash replied.

They waited, the cold increased. Eventually they had to keep their fingers from getting stiff by putting them in coat pockets.

Caleb proved to have more patience than his companion. He sat hunched and watchful as time passed. Ash, unaccustomed to long periods of inactivity, was almost pleased when distant gunfire reached them. He and the old man's son were on their feet in moments, stiffness only impaired their progress back the way they had come until their blood was pumping, then Ash had to follow Caleb at a steady trot.

When they were nearing stump country where the logs had been cut for the Wolff buildings, Ash caught Caleb's arm and made a statement. "There must be another trail."

If Caleb intended to reply brisking up gunfire kept him from doing so. He led off again, and this time there was moonlight. Ash followed but warily. Movement would make them visible the closer they got to the edge of the stump country. This time when Caleb stopped they could make out the house.

The old man was firing back, but the intervals between shots told Ash that the old man's rifle was a single-shot weapon.

Caleb would have started forward but Ash caught his arm and jerked his head. This time Ash did the leading. He went easterly at the same time he angled until they were back among tall trees.

The gunfire slackened, then stopped altogether. Ash guessed the attackers were also reloading. When Caleb would have spoken Ash held up his hand for silence. From this point on he led warily. What he thought he had heard during the lull was a horse stamping.

Against the probability that the attackers would have left someone to mind the horses, Ash went northerly deeper into the timber before beginning a stealthy stalk southward.

Caleb finally understood Ash's intention and followed close. Ash halted beside a huge old cedar tree and pointed.

Four horses stood in a group where they had been tethered.

Ash waited until the fight brisked up again and made straight for the horses. Caleb hung back a short way holding his handgun, but there was no one with the animals.

They got among the animals, who accepted their presence with the fatalism of horses. He did not untie the animals, Ash used a razor-sharp clasp knife to cut the reins up close to the bits.

When the firing resumed Ash and Caleb spooked the horses, they scattered in the darkness.

Ash went ahead until he could see the buildings again, motioned for Caleb to go eastward, after which they began their stalk.

They could clearly see muzzle blast from the house but the attackers were firing weapons that showed no muzzle blast. Ash stopped. Within moments a lumpy shape no more than a hundred feet ahead hunched around to reload.

Ash widened his stride, and when

other attackers fired again, he came up beside the reloading man and swung his six-gun. The man crumpled, his half-reloaded carbine clattering among rocks.

When he looked around Caleb was grinning. He would not see that expression on the old man's son's face again for a long time.

Locating another attacker was more difficult. He was among the stumps, out where Ash and Caleb could not go because they would be discernible when they moved.

Caleb picked up a fist-sized rock and began stalking the man facing the house. He was still some distance away when his father fired from the house and pieces of punky wood flew in all directions from the attacker's stump.

He sprang up racing to get back among the trees. Caleb was ready. As the man flashed past Caleb caught him by the arm and hurled the rock.

The attacker had no chance to avoid being struck. He and the old man's son were very close to each other, but this attacker yelled seconds before the rock struck his forehead.

The gunfire stopped. During a long lull the old man fired again, after which the silence returned. Caleb twisted to go in pursuit but Ash caught him by the shoulder and whirled him until they were facing, then he said, "The hell with 'em."

They went far around to the west keeping the house in sight. When there was no more shooting and they were close enough to sprint toward the house, Ash led off.

The old man saw two running wraiths and in his haste to reload, dropped his powder horn. They could hear his profanity yards before they reached the log walls.

Caleb went around behind the house with Ash following. There was adequate moonlight to see the door. Caleb reached the porch and grasped the latch. When he flung the door inward the old man was standing in the centre of the room gripping his rifle in both hands to use as a club. Lisa called sharply. The old man did not change his stance until both his son and Ash Fitzhugh were inside, then he flung the rifle aside and in a surprisingly normal voice told his daughter to fetch the jug.

The only window of glass was in the front wall. The log wall had absorbed most of the gunfire but the parlour had not escaped damage from the shattered window.

Caleb leaned aside his Winchester, methodically went to the stove to chuck in two more scantlings, then turned. His father said, "Boy, I come within an ace of brainin' you."

Caleb had not been in any danger but he nodded as his sister brought whiskey. She barely acknowledged the presence of Ash as she poured into three cups, but the old man did. He said, "Nolan's a coyote son of a bitch. You boys done us proud."

No one added to that. Lisa, in

womanly fashion, set about doing what she could to set things to rights. Caleb told the old man what they had done and the old man smiled from ear to ear. He sank into a chair looking from his son to Ash. He wagged his head as he said, "I figured they'd bypassed you boys when the shootin' commenced. I worried they'd find you." He sipped for a moment then wagged his head again watching fire brighten in the stove. "Mister Fitzhugh . . . "

Ash moved the rifle to make a place for him to sit. He said nothing.

The old man resumed speaking. "Mister Fitzhugh, you're both a curse an' a blessing." He gazed at the couch where Ash was sitting. "That was close."

Caleb stood with his back to the stove. "It had to come," he told his father, "an' for my part I'm glad it did." Caleb jerked his head in Ash's direction. "Mister Fitzhugh's a good man to ride the rims with."

For the first time Lisa spoke.

"There's a bullet hole in Ma's picture."

The old man said, "Turn up the lamp, girl. Where?"

"Low in front. I'll patch it."

The old man sat rumpled and sprawling gazing at the picture of his wife above a small table where a lighted lamp stood. He raised his cup. "Allie, you done right proud too. You always was somethin' I could count on."

Lisa dropped into a chair, hands lying in her lap like dead birds. She gazed at the shattered window. Her father had told her he had given it to her mother one Christmas. Glass was scarce and expensive. Her mother had helped her father cut the square in the front wall and install the window. She turned to her brother. "Did you kill the two you caught?"

Caleb didn't think so, "Ash busted the first one over the head. I caught the other one in the head with a rock. In the mornin' we'll look for 'em."

The old man strongly said, "You don't do no such a thing. Nolan'll be on the warpath now, for a fact. All of us got to stay close." The old man's gaze drifted around to Ash. "At least until tomorrow night."

Ash and the old man exchanged a bleak smile.

4

When the Iron's Hot!

ASH humoured the old man as did his son and daughter, but there was not the tie between them there was with the old man's offspring.

He went outside where cold air hit him full force, and breathed deeply. That was something he would learn, if he lived long enough. Idaho's cold night air cleared cobwebs from a man's mind in minutes.

While he was out there Caleb came. He was not allowed to have a spittoon in the house. He let fly once, ran a work-roughened hand over his mouth and said, "I don't think Nolan will be back. Those two we caught won't be in shape for much ridin' for a while. They might even quit. If I was one of them I sure as hell would. Fightin' a range war where a man could get killed, wages an' keep wouldn't be enough."

For Caleb Wolff it had been a long statement. Ash studied the stars in long silence. Eventually he said, "We whittled down the odds."

"For a fact, an' it's two miles on foot to get back."

Ash ignored that and continued to study the heavens. "You ever heard it said that the best time to hit is when the iron's hot?"

Caleb put a puzzled look on Ash. "What're you talkin' about?"

Ash lowered his gaze. "Two miles isn't much of a hike, an' you know the way."

Caleb's eyes narrowed at Ash. "Pa will have a fit. You heard what he said about stayin' close."

"I heard. They brought the fight here. It's natural for us to take it back to them."

"Now?"

"Now!"

Caleb sprayed amber, scratched his beard and did not speak for a long time. Then he said, "Pa — "

"We go without tellin' him."

Again Caleb ruminated. "Maybe tomorrow night. Ash?"

"Caleb, by tomorrow night they'll be figurin' we might do somethin'."

Caleb's problem was simply that although he wanted to fight fire with fire, for years he had followed the old man's edicts about wearing Nolan down. He had never agreed, which had made him the frustrated man he had become. But he had lived a long time under the old man's domination. He finally muttered, "I don't know."

Ash responded a little irritably, "Don't ponder too long or it'll be too late to hike two miles. We can't do it after daylight."

Caleb said, "Our Winchesters are inside an' we ought to take along plenty of bullets."

Ash smiled. "We go back inside. I'll try to get your pa into the kitchen.

You get the carbines and some shells an' come back out here. As soon as I can come back we'll leave."

Perhaps if the lighting had been better, or Lisa and the old man hadn't been preoccupied with patching the hole in Lisa's mother's picture, either she or the old man would have suspected something, because Caleb's face was set in an unusual expression. But they noticed nothing and when the patching had been completed to Lisa's satisfaction she went to the kitchen to move the coffee pot to a burner. She did not like coffee, but her menfolk did, and she knew from observation that Ash also did.

She was surprised when Ash came to the kitchen doorway and lingered. She looked up once then became busy arranging fat wood in the kindling box.

Ash studied the room with its cupboards made out of wooden crates, its sink and drainboard made of roughly planed wood. There were two stoves, the large iron one for cooking, the much smaller one for warming the room.

Ash stood in the front of the doorless cupboards looking for the whiskey crock. Lisa said, "Are you hungry?"

His reply was quietly given as he looked at her. "No ma'am. I was lookin' for the jug. I figured your pa'n me could set here at the table an' have a cup of Irish coffee."

She accepted that with no reason not to, went to the doorway and while drying her hands on an apron, called to her father.

The old man came, saw Ash and pulled out a chair at the kitchen table as his daughter put two cups of coffee there. The old man looked up at Ash. "What you lookin' for?"

"The jug. I been cold so long just coffee won't work."

Will Wolff arose, went around the farthest cupboard, leaned down and straightened up with the jug. As he returned to the table he said, "Three times I've had 'em get broke from bein' on a shelf." He filled Ash's cup to the brim, did the same with his own cup and looked across the table. "If you'n Caleb hurt Nolan's riders, I expect he'll have to go all the way to Wildroot to hire replacements." The old man sipped, put the cup down and leaned on the table. "What happened tonight . . . I can't recall anyone doin' to Mister Nolan what was done tonight. He dassn't let the word get around or he'll have other folks standin' up to him. All the same, if it hadn't happened — "

Lisa cut in, "Cal an' me never believed like you. We never felt we could wait Mister Nolan out."

The old man sipped again and wagged his shaggy head. "I'm tired. I ain't used to all this excitement. I think I'll bed down."

Ash arose, watched the old man leave the room, reached for his cup, emptied it and started to leave the kitchen. Lisa stopped him in the doorway, head slightly to one side.

"Where's my brother?" she asked.

"Maybe down at the barn. I don't know," Ash replied, beginning to feel uncomfortable the way she was watching him.

"Mister Fitzhugh, I don't know you but I know my brother." She paused. "You come into the kitchen lookin' at the shelves. You never did that before. Cal should have been here. Where is he?"

He heard a bedroom door slam and regarded her steadily. She was pretty and intense. Instinct told him not to lie to her. He said, "Don't wake your pa."

"Why not?"

"Your brother an' I are goin' to the Nolan place."

"What!"

"Take the fight to them."

She put a hand to her lips with widening eyes. For a moment she simply stared, then she said, "No! You can't do — "

68

"Why can't we? Lisa, Nolan's got two hurt riders, that brings the odds pretty close to even, an' the idea is to hit him now, not set an' wait for him to come back over here."

She went to the table and sat down without taking her eyes off him. "You could get killed. You'n my brother."

"You think after what we did tonight when Nolan comes back he'll just shoot up the yard? He'll come back for blood. Caleb'n I figure to hit while the iron's hot. If we don't, if we set an' wait, sure as you're sittin' there he'll kill your pa an' your brother. Lisa, all I ask is that you let your pa have a good night's sleep. Now I got to go."

"Where's my brother?"

"Out back waitin' for me."

She left the chair, whipped past Ash, through the parlour and flung the door open. Caleb gave an owlish stare, saw Ash behind her and neither moved nor spoke.

For a moment the brother and sister simply stared at each other then Lisa went forward, stood on her tiptoes and kissed her brother. As she settled down she said, "Be careful."

Caleb nodded without speaking. Ash got around her, took the Winchester Caleb handed him, pocketed the loose cartridges too and smiled at the girl.

She remained in the doorway until her brother and Ash Fitzhugh passed from sight around the south-west corner of the house.

It was cold, the sky was brilliant, the moon looked like freshly minted silver. The old dog came from his home beneath the porch and watched. So did Lisa, from the shattered front-wall window over which she had hung a blanket.

Caleb walked with a purposeful stride, neither stopped nor looked back. When they reached timber they had to sashay among the trees, Caleb did this like someone who knew every yard of the area, which he did.

An owl almost as large as a turkey

swooped soundlessly. They had only a glimpse as it winged eastward to find another perch.

The timber was not only thick it was deep. They had hiked the better part of an hour before Ash could make out faint moonlight ahead. He had no idea how long they had been on the trail, nor did that bother him.

He scented cattle but did not see them. They were bedded down near a westerly creek. If they caught human scent they were not troubled by it, so it must have seemed distant, which it was.

The needle-covered ground muffled sound but as they continued ahead in the direction of that filtered moonlight, the country changed; there were rocks, mostly no larger than a fist, but also huge old plinths, dark at night and also during day. Lava rock is always dark, sometimes it is pocked and light to lift, but not those plinths, they had struck the earth millions of years ago, fired from a volcano that no longer existed.

They were buried at least three feet in the stony soil.

Caleb finally stopped. He was facing open country where small bosques of trees stood. Ash saw the buildings about a quarter-mile ahead, and was impressed. Nolan had a number of log outbuildings, almost a spider web of sorting and marking corrals. The barn was taller than most for a simple reason, Nolan kept at least a dozen using horses in the corrals at all times. That high loft was full of hay.

The main house was not much larger than the Wolff place. It had a covered porch completely around. There were no flowers or shrubs. Ash asked Caleb if Nolan was married and got a shake of the bearded man's head. A dog barked, not excitedly because the scents were too distant. Caleb turned his head. "He's got more'n one dog. They're goin' to be a problem."

The bunkhouse had a covered porch out front. Caleb identified and studied it. He said, "There's two hurt fellers in there. That leaves Fred and one rider. Maybe we ought to try for the bunkhouse first."

Ash was more interested in the main house. There was not a light showing anywhere. "How close can we get to the main house?"

"From behind, except for the dogs we ought to be able to make it."

Every ranch Ash had known had dogs. They kept varmints away, announced the arrival of strangers, helped work cattle. As a rule they lived in the yard and because they were rarely petted had testy dispositions. The dilemma for Ash and the old man's son was to avoid arousing the dogs, but neither man believed that could be done. Caleb leaned his carbine aside to blow on his hands. Ash said, "Do you know the main house?"

"I never been beyond the porch. Why? Make a run for it an' to hell with the dogs?"

"No. One of us go around westerly toward the barn an' corrals, the other one'll head for the back of the house. If the dogs scent up the one sneakin' around to the barn they'll raise a ruckus down there."

Caleb looked at his companion. "Mind me askin' a personal question?" he asked.

Ash said, "After we're on our way back." He thought he knew what the question would be and had no intention of allowing it to be asked, nor answered.

Caleb picked up the carbine. "I'll draw 'em to the barn." He paused. "Maybe I'd ought to tell you somethin'. Fred Nolan isn't a big man but he's hell on wheels. A dead shot and got a mean streak down his back a foot wide. If you get inside, don't give the son of a bitch a chance."

Ash nodded. "I hope you make it to the barn before the dogs do." Caleb sidled westerly keeping to what little cover there was, until he was in a direct line with the barn and corrals. He looked back once. Ash nodded.

The distance Caleb had to cover had to be measured in yards. He did not hasten and carried the saddlegun in both hands.

Ash waited for the dogs to pick up the scent, but there was a slight breeze blowing from the east. Caleb was out of sight, close to the outbuildings, when the dogs sounded. It seemed like a pack of them. In fact there were only five, but with the strange scent the noise sounded like a dozen dogs.

Ash started for the main house. The dogs probably wouldn't have scented him, not only because they were raising hell and propping it up in the area of the barn, but also because Ash was approaching from the south with the main house dead ahead to block both a scenting and a sighting.

He did not see the bunkhouse lamp sputter to life before he reached the back of the Nolan residence. He tried to detect sound inside but the dogs made it impossible for anything to be heard but their barking.

Every residence had a back door and the Nolan place was no exception, but it was a massively sturdy door with heavy hand-wrought hinges, and was barred from the inside. If a man tried shooting his way inside he'd need either a cannon or a Gatling gun.

There was no time to respect the cowman's precautions against being raided. Ash sidled along the wall feeling for windows, any kind of opening. What he eventually found, around the corner along the east wall, was a shuttered window open about six or seven inches at the bottom. He thought it would be a bedroom; men who lived and worked in the open rarely slept in rooms where fresh air could not penetrate.

He tested the shutters. They were latched on the inside. He dug out his knife, got the largest blade between the shutters and carefully lifted. He heard the latch drop and hoped that Mister Nolan was a deep sleeper. He waited. Nothing happened; there was no sound from the inside. He eased up a hand to push one of the shutters inward. It did not make a sound as it yielded. He started to ease the other one open and probably because it hadn't been opened in a long time, it squeaked.

Ash stopped pushing. He could, with some difficulty, get inside without having both shutters open. He used both hands to raise the window, and it did not move. He exerted effort and it still did not budge. He paused and stepped back to study the window. It was made to slide upwards. What he had encountered was one of those windows everyone encounters one time or another that, having not been raised, had been swollen by rain until both sides were wedged to the jam.

He was losing time. The dogs were still sounding. He went on around to the east wall where there was a door and some neatly piled kindling wood, but whoever had installed this door had put the hinges on the outside. They were the draw-bolt variety. The door would open outward.

Ash used his knife to raise the topmost bolt. Probably because the porch was covered it was not rusted and came out with a minimum of prying, but the bottom bolt had been wedged when the top bolt had come out, so Ash had to lean against the door to achieve enough purchase to pry out the lower bolt. When this happened the door struck the outer wall at the bottom. It would have made enough noise to rouse a sleeper except for the agitated barking in the area of the barn.

Ash lifted it aside and leaned it carefully against the wall.

Inside, there was enough darkness to force him to wait for his eyes to adjust before entering.

The kitchen was large and well kept, something rare in the dwellings of single men. It smelled of cooking. Ahead was the doorless opening into the parlour. Ash did not hesitate, time was passing and Caleb could not avoid trouble indefinitely.

The parlour was large, its leather furniture adequate for the size of the room, and it was dark. What little moonlight came through a front window did not do much to dispel the gloom.

There was a large stone fireplace, several guns in corners, and Ash started stealthily in the direction of a hallway running east and west, on his way to the bedroom with the immovable window. He was never afterward to say whether it was instinct or a sound that made him spring sideways and flatten against the wall.

He waited, heart pounding. He waited for a repetition of the sound, if indeed that was what had startled him, before moving clear of the wall to go in the direction of that gloomy hallway, and this time his heart stopped for a fraction of a second before the muzzle-blast and explosion nearly deafened and blinded him.

He had seen neither the gun or the man holding it. Before he could draw his own sidearm an apparition emerged from the hallway and this time he caught weak moonlight off the gun swinging in his direction.

He drew and fired. The wraith in a light-coloured nightshirt fired back. Ash felt the sting and the warm flow of blood. He had been notched in either his left arm or under it, along the ribs.

He hesitated, the shock caused seconds of delay. The wraith, short and moving ghost-like fired again. This time something made of glass on Ash's right shattered. The smell of coal oil spread almost instantly.

Ash blended, the man in the light-coloured nightshirt did not, but he moved as Ash fired, evidently struck a low table and the wraith's next shot went ceilingward.

Ash launched himself, gun rising for a blow. The shorter man would not regain his balance in time before the larger, heavier man struck him. But what Caleb had warned Ash about was true; the shorter man fought like a tiger. When Ash hit his gun hand with a balled fist the weapon skidded across the floor.

The man used bony fists, knees, even his legs. Once, he raised up high enough to bite Ash's ear and again there was the sensation of warm blood. Ash tried several times to nail the man with his fists and missed each time. It was like wrestling with a greased pig. His adversary bucked and twisted and struck out. He never stopped moving. He was wiry, fast and arched hard enough to throw Ash off balance. As he instinctively reached out to prevent falling, the short man kicked viciously and broke clear. He was quicker to get upright than Ash was, but as he jumped past for his six-gun Ash reached with both hands for an ankle, and got it. The shorter man twisted to kick savagely with his free leg. The blow caught Ash in the ribs, pain shot through him but he clung to the ankle and raised up enough to wrench as hard as he could. As the other man sprawled Ash got to his feet, put a booted foot down on the wrist groping for the gun, and leaned to hold his adversary, when the short man roared a curse and rolled clear to spring to his feet.

Ash stopped. They faced each other in the darkness, neither man able to see much more of the other than his outline and a few details.

Ash raised his six-gun and cocked it.

The short man eyed the gun, went to a chair and sat down.

Ash picked up the short man's six-gun and tossed it into his lap, then waited. But the man in the chair was anything but a fool. He tossed the gun to the floor. He said, "I'm not sure but I think I know who you are, an' I'll pay you three times the goin' rate if you'll work for me."

Ash had pain, he was bleeding, his shirt was torn. He stood motionless looking at the other man as he said,

"Is your name Nolan?"

"Yes. What's yours?"

Ash leaned against a table, his heart was pounding and he was sucking air. The man in the nightshirt seemed not to be breathing hard, or if he was it didn't show when he spoke, and he did not raise his voice. Ash eyed Fred Nolan; Caleb had been right but only marginally so, the short man had just fought for his life and now, sitting in the red leather chair, he sounded like someone who was interviewing a prospective rangeman. Nolan was unlike any man Ash had ever known.

The seated man spoke again. "Was you one of the men who caught my boys over at the squatter's place?"

Ash pulled down a big breath and exhaled. "I'll go with you to get your pants. Get up."

"All right, five times the goin' wage."

"*Get up!* Walk ahead of me an' if you so much as miss a step I'll kill you. *Walk!*"

Nolan walked, turned into the

83

bedroom where light entered past the opened shutters and without another word or even a glance at Ash dressed himself. He faced around. Ash jerked his head for Nolan to return to the hallway and growled at him which direction to take until they came to the heavy door with a drawbar across it set in two steel hangers.

Ash said, "Open it."

As Nolan was obeying he said, "If you think you're goin' to take me away from here, you're a fool. Those dogs rousted out the men in the bunkhouse."

Nolan leaned the drawbar aside and faced Ash, who shook his head. If the short man knew what fear was he certainly did not act like he did.

Before Ash gave his next order he stood appraising Fred Nolan and coming to the conclusion that all he'd heard was not only true, but a whole lot Ash had never heard would also be true.

He said, "Go outside, turn right and

stop at the corner of the house."

Again Nolan obeyed to the letter. The dogs were still snarling, barking, making excited runs at the barn.

When Ash started to speak Nolan beat him to it. "Who's with you? Mister, you're a damned fool if you figure we're goin' to walk across the yard, me in front, you behind with a gun, and reach the yard."

Ash wagged his head. "You got one rider, the other two got hurt pretty bad. We'll walk side by side to the barn, when we get there call off those dogs."

Nolan snorted. The dogs were excited beyond any man's control.

5

A Time for Decision

TWO dogs were inside the barn, three made runs at the doorless wide opening unwilling to go farther. When they saw two men approaching they turned their fury on the walkers. Nolan snarled, one dog slunk away but the remaining two began a stiff-legged circling movement, hackles up, fangs bared.

Nolan stopped as though to pick up a rock and both dogs fled.

When the two men appeared in the barn opening both dogs inside were at the base of the loft ladder and did not see the newcomers until Nolan snarled, then they turned. They acted bewildered. Nolan swore and they ran out the rear opening. For the first time in an hour there was no barking.

Ash called and Caleb answered from the loft.

Ash said, "Come down. I got Mister Nolan with me."

"Are them dogs gone?"

"They're gone, climb down."

Caleb appeared in the loft hole, turned and came down backwards. When he was on the ground he and Nolan exchanged a sulphurous glare until Ash told Caleb to bring in three horses from out back.

As Caleb turned, someone in the dark up front cocked a gun.

Ash gave the shorter man a violent shove that sent Nolan sprawling.

Two guns went off simultaneously, one from out front, the other from near the rear opening. Both Ash and Nolan were temporarily blinded. Caleb appeared soundlessly heading for the front opening. Before he got there a man began swearing and growling. Caleb called to him. "Get where I can see you!"

"Can't stand up," the man said.

"Then crawl you son of a bitch!"

Ash heard someone out front dragging himself. When the crawling man came into view Ash recognized him; he was the Nolan rider calling himself Bill Jones.

Caleb abruptly swung and growled. "Take another step, Mister Nolan, an' I'll blow your damned head off!"

Ash's sight was returning. Caleb started toward the man who had stopped crawling, stood over him and aimed his Colt directly at the man's head. "Stand up!"

"I can't. Lend me a hand."

Caleb said, "Ash, help him up."

As Ash went forward Caleb spoke again. "You better not have a gun."

The man groaned. Ash went close, lifted him upright and the man reached to hold Ash. "My leg's broke," he exclaimed.

Caleb whirled and fired a shot toward the rear opening and Nolan stopped dead in his tracks with both arms raised.

Caleb snarled for the short man to come back up front, which Nolan did, and Ash hit him with a rock-hard fist. Nolan collapsed and Caleb said, "Mind 'em," to Ash and went out back for horses.

The laconic, hard-faced man who had said his name was Bill Jones was grinding his teeth. Ash ignored that to ask about the other two Nolan riders. Jones replied through clenched teeth, "They quit an' rode off headin' for Wildroot an' a doctor."

Nolan rolled up into a crouch looking up. Ash told him to lie belly down and not to move.

It required nearly a half-hour to get the horses rigged and when they were ready Bill Jones said he couldn't ride. Even in darkness they could see his right trouser soaked with blood. Jones looked at Nolan. "Measly bunch of squatters is they?"

Nolan said nothing so Jones spoke again. "Give me the money in your pocket. When I'm able I'll come back'n slit your pouch an' pull your leg through it. *The money!*"

Neither Ash nor Caleb interrupted so Nolan dug out a roll of greenbacks and handed it to Jones.

Caleb tied one saddled horse to a stud-ring and told Jones it'd be there when he was able to ride, then he faced Nolan. "Get astride. I hate your guts. I hope you give me a chance to kill you. Now get up there an' don't move."

The three of them rode out of the yard to the tune of dogs barking, to which they paid no attention. They rode with Nolan between them. One look at Caleb's profile was enough to prevent Ash from asking how he had made that shot that hit Jones in the leg.

It was cold; when they got into the timber they put Nolan a horse length in front and followed the route he used in and out among the trees.

While they were still in timber Nolan asked a question without turning his head. "Where are we goin'?"

Caleb answered surlily, "Shut up!"

That ended all talk as the chill steadily increased as it always did before dawn.

The graze on the inside of Ash's arm didn't amount to much, but the kick in the ribs was painful. Every step of the horse made Ash suck air.

His collar was wet where he had been bitten, but except for a mild aching sensation, what bothered him was how quickly the blood on his shoulder got cold.

They were nearing the stump country when Caleb addressed Nolan's back. "One way or another I'm goin' to kill you, you miserable son of a bitch!"

Nolan acted as though he had heard nothing and through his pain Ash developed a grudging and reluctant respect for the short man.

They finally came to clear country. The moon was gone so they rode by starlight. For Caleb the direction was as fixed in his mind as it had been since his pa had brought him to this area. He growled once for Nolan to watch for light but Nolan also knew the area; he was being taken to the Wolff place. What his thoughts were was anyone's guess, but surely one of them had to do with his present predicament and how it had come about. Feared and hated for miles in all directions, Nolan's humiliation included thoughts about how news of this night would spread.

The light was weak and distant. Weak because darkness was yielding to the sickly grey of a predawn morning.

Ash did not begin to feel exhausted until they were crossing the meadow in the direction of the barn. When they halted out front to dump horse gear before leading the animals inside, Ash thought about the old man's grain squeezings and that kept him moving when they finally began their march toward the house.

Lisa heard them mount the porch steps and flung the door open. She was temporarily frightened. She had

Mister Nolan less than five feet away staring at her. Caleb gave Nolan a shove, Lisa closed the door after the men and remained leaning on it as Caleb punched Nolan into his father's favourite chair before joining Ash in pouring barrel-cured whiskey into two cups.

Ash went to stand by the stove, the heat worked through his clothes.

Lisa came over, big-eyed, as she almost whispered, "How bad is it?"

Ash regarded her from brightening eyes when he replied, "He's a lousy shot in the dark. I'll be all right in a day or two."

She was not convinced, "I'll get the medicine satchel."

When the men were alone Caleb sat directly opposite Fred Nolan with whiskey warming him. "When we been here a few years we built up a little herd."

Nolan interrupted, "You'll get 'em back."

Caleb's eyes were narrowed as he

93

regarded the shorter man. "Twenty-eight cows an' a Durham bull. In the years since you stole 'em, them cows'll have calved quite a few times. You understand what I'm aimin' at, Mister Nolan?"

"I told you, you'll get 'em back."

Caleb nodded solemnly. "When I can get a pencil an' some paper I'll figure out how many calves they've had."

Nolan's testiness surfaced. "I told you, you'll get all your cattle back."

Caleb did not look away nor change his tone of voice when he said, "Somethin' happened to our horses. You know anythin' about that?"

Nolan looked at Ash and bobbed his head toward the jug. Ash crossed to hand it to Nolan when Caleb sprang up cursing and would have grabbed for the mug but Ash swung it hard. Caleb staggered. Ash said, "Set down!"

He handed the jug to Mister Nolan, who swung it to one shoulder, turned his head and swallowed. As he was

94

lowering the jug he looked at Ash. "Is this some of Will Wolff's whiskey, because if it is it's the smoothest I ever tasted."

Neither Lisa, Caleb nor Ash were impressed. Caleb said, "Before I hang you in the yard, you can have all you want."

There was a bear-like groan from the open doorway beside the stove as Will Wolff appeared, clad in shirt and britches and old boots. His hair looked like it had been combed by a hay rake. When the shock of seeing who was sitting in his favourite chair passed, the old man came forward. He was looking at Caleb when he said, "You boys went over there an' caught the son of a bitch?"

Ash answered because Caleb was silently glaring. "Wasn't much trouble. I've been in worse fixes."

The old man scratched inside his shirt. "Mister Nolan," he said in a growly drawl and paused to wag his head. "I never figured I'd have you settin' in my parlour."

Nolan eyed the old man sceptically. "I told your boy you'd get the cattle back."

"Well now, that's right neighbourly of you. An' what about the horses, we get them back too?"

"Ones just as good, Mister Wolff."

"It's *Mister* Wolff is it?" The old man dragged a chair and sat. "I expect there's other things, like that glass winder. I paid three dollars on the barrel head because my wife wanted somethin' nice."

Ash could see the testiness in Nolan's face and headed it off with a question. "You expect to go to that town an' hire new riders?"

Before Nolan could reply Caleb spoke. "Only place he's goin' is as far as the old cottonwood with that branch that sticks straight out."

His father turned and shook his head. "Boy, Mister Nolan's our guest."

Caleb growled, opened the stove door, expectorated and closed the door.

The old man faced their hostage but said nothing for a long time, then he arose, tipped whiskey into a cup and handed it to Nolan, who said, "Thanks," and briefly tipped the cup, then set it aside as he eyed the old man, who seemed close to smiling when he spoke again.

"You see that picture of my wife?"

Nolan looked and turned back.

"Mister Nolan, you or one of your hired hands shot a hole in that picture, and let me tell you, I take that real personal. She was as fine a woman as Gawd put on this earth."

Nolan's eyes narrowed a fraction as he regarded the old man in silence.

"If I was to add up shootin' into the yard, poisonin' my horses, creatin' every kind of hardship you could to run us off, in greenbacks it'd be a considerable amount. You understand me?"

Nolan glanced at Caleb and back to the old man. Caleb's fixed expression since before they had come to the house was murderous. Even Lisa was regarding the rancher with a cold, bleak expression. Only the tall stranger with the bloody shirt did not regard Nolan with hatred. Nolan emptied the cup, looked at the old man and said, "Mister Wolff, right now you got the upper hand, but that'll change when I — "

The old man came out of his chair in one bound, stepped directly in front of Nolan, got a handful of shirting and with his face close he said, "You never had the upper hand. All you done was pile up big debt for us to get payment for." He released Nolan's shirt and straightened up. "If I liked hangin' you, you son of a bitch, I'd go fetch that new length of rope we brought back from Wildroot." The old man paused. He and Nolan had glances locked on each other. "But I've seen lynchings an' the idea goes against my beliefs."

Nolan's reply was testy. "That's good, Mister Wolff, because you'd never get away with it."

For Caleb that was the last straw, he came from over by the stove six-gun in hand. He raised and aimed it from a distance of no more than three feet. When he cocked it Ash held his breath.

Nolan looked straight at Caleb without blinking. "I said I'd bring the cattle back an' replace the horses. I said I'll leave you folks alone." Nolan paused for breath. "As for payin' money, I'll do that too. Now then, you pull that trigger an' you'll get nothin'. With me dead there'll be other stockmen in need of graze, an' believe me, they'll come an' when they do you'll be worse off than you have been."

Ash still held his breath. It was Lisa who spoke next. "Caleb, put up the gun! I want him dead too, but killing him won't change things."

The old man softly said, "Put it up, boy," and Caleb eased the hammer down, leathered his Colt and returned to his place by the stove.

The old man was shrewd. A person could not live as long as he had without getting that way. When it seemed this affair was going to end Caleb growled from over by the stove. "Pa, his promise ain't worth the breath it took to give it."

The old man raised an arm in the direction of his son and Caleb said no more. Ash was breathing again, he had no particular objection to lynchings, but he did not believe in shooting an unarmed man sitting in a chair.

Nolan addressed the old man in a voice indicating he had not just been as close to death as a person could get. He didn't know the old man very well. In fact he knew none of his captors very well, the tall man who had whipped him least of all.

He held out his empty cup. The old man tipped in a little more. Nolan swallowed twice and put the cup aside, looking straight at the old man. The whiskey was undoubtedly working on him. He said, "If you'll step out on the porch with me for a few minutes," and arose.

Caleb started moving. This time it was Ash who stopped him. He flung out an arm with a closed fist at the end of it. Caleb stepped back in front of the stove, but he growled, "Don't do it, Pa. That bastard's as slippery as a greased pole."

The old man stood up as though his son had not spoken. As he passed, Ash handed the old man his six-gun. The old man shoved it in the front of his britches and followed Nolan out into the first light of day. It was cold but the men on the porch were sufficiently warm.

Nolan gestured toward a chair and sat down in one close by. He waited until the old man was seated and had made the necessary adjustment any man had to make if he had a six-gun shoved down the front of his britches.

Nolan said, "I don't apologize for

anything. I ran stock over your place before you come into the country. Scarin' you out didn't work. Buyin' you out didn't work either. But I'm goin' to make you another offer. Six thousand dollars for a quit claim an' you move on."

The old man cleared his throat. He had never known that much money in his lifetime. And for a fact his holdings weren't worth more than $500. $800 or $1,000 at the very most counting improvements and a cabin-high stack of winter wood.

The old man eased back in the chair looking northward. He had always liked the view from the porch. He said, "Six thousand dollars?"

"On the barrel head. I'll fetch it from the bank in Wildroot."

The old man slowly arose and with his back to the stockman watched a stray beam of sunlight pass through the treetops and land squarely on his wife's grave.

Nolan said, "It's cold out here."

The old man neither commented nor faced around. He told himself he knew what she would say — take it and find an even nicer place.

Nolan's impatience drove him back inside where Caleb challenged him. "Where's my pa?"

"On the porch."

Caleb brushed roughly past and went out there, slamming the door after himself.

His father hadn't moved but that sliver of brilliant ray of sunlight had. It no longer shone on the grave.

The old man turned. "He'll give us six thousand for the place, Caleb."

The burly, bearded man was stunned. "You sure that's what he said? Pa, your hearin' ain't been real good lately."

"He said six thousand dollars, Caleb. He was settin' right next to me. I know that's what he said."

Caleb groped for a chair and sat down. "He's up to somethin'. He wants to get away, go round up some rangemen an' come back loaded for bear."

"Caleb . . . I don't think so. He meant it. Six *thousand* dollars! I'm goin' inside. I need some stiffenin'."

Caleb didn't move. "It ain't worth one thousand," he said.

The old man was quiet for a spell then faced around. "Boy, I'll tell you somethin' you wouldn't know for another forty, fifty years. I can't do it. Your ma's over yonder."

Caleb said nothing.

"But I'll take the money, you can have half, Lisa can have half, an' the pair of you can go out in the world. Me, I'll stay."

"He won't let you stay, Pa."

"Yes he will, otherwise he can keep his six thousand dollars."

As the old man went toward the door Caleb arose to follow.

6

Wildroot

SOMEONE had fed the stove. It was almost too hot. Ash, Lisa and Nolan had been sitting in silence. They looked around when Caleb and his father entered. Each face had a strained expression.

The old man went to the chair opposite Nolan, sat down, clasped his hands and nodded. Nolan said, "I'll ride to Wildroot in the mornin' an' fetch back the money."

Lisa looked bewildered. "Pa, you're sellin' out to him?"

The old man looked directly at Fred Nolan. "One thing. I got to stay."

Nolan scowled. "I want the place empty."

The old man considered Nolan pensively. "My wife's buried out yonder. That won't mean nothin' to you but it means an awful lot to me. You can have the place but I stay."

Nolan's scowl lingered. Before he could speak Lisa spoke again, "Pa!"

The old man faced his daughter. "It ain't fair keepin' you'n Caleb here. You're both young. You deserve better'n livin' up here, an' you'll have enough money to set up somewhere else. Maybe not so far from towns."

Caleb's baleful gaze was fixed on Nolan. "I'll ride with you to Wildroot."

Nolan shrugged. Ash spoke after his long silence. "I'll go, Caleb."

The old man cut across Caleb's forming objection. His reason was the same reason Ash had volunteered. Caleb hated Fred Nolan and accidents happen. "Ash'll go, Caleb. You'n me can ride lookin' for cattle."

Caleb spoke sharply — and truthfully — to his father. "What good'll cattle be if we got no land to run 'em on?"

Nolan looked directly at Caleb when he said, "I said I'd pay you, an' that means for the cattle too."

The old man stood up. He was a formidable figure, ruggedly old and strong. "We'll take your offer, Mister Nolan." He looked enquiringly at Nolan, who nodded and also stood up. Nolan asked if Ash had a blanket roll. Ash had, so Nolan addressed the old man, "If we set out now we can damn near make it come tomorrow night."

Caleb remained behind but Lisa went with the men to the barn where horses were saddled in silence. As he mounted outside near the tie rack Nolan spoke to the old man. He seemed to have been thinking. He said, "You're a hard trader, Mister Wolff," and the old man made a weary smile.

From the porch Lisa watched the riders leave the yard. When her father joined her, Lisa looked up round eyed. "Cal said six thousand dollars."

The old man nodded, groped for a chair and sat down. The dog who lived under the porch came up to sit beside him. Caleb went down to the barn where the remaining horse required care. Lisa perched on the porch railing looking at her father. "What about Ma?"

"That's why I'm stayin'," the old man replied, and smiled. Lisa had been his favourite but he'd never let it show. "I'm old, nothin' much matters any more, least of all money. Your ma an' I was married a lot of years. Good years. I wouldn't sleep nights with strangers out yonder."

Lisa went inside to prepare a meal, the old man and the old dog remained in warm sunshine and shade.

Along toward high noon the day turned off hot. Nolan and Ash bypassed the Nolan yard and rode over miles of some of the best graze Ash had ever seen, all of it west of the broken country.

The trail to Wildroot was well marked and dusty, in places it was a tad narrow with steep drop-offs on both sides. Nolan led the way. Quiet and thoughtful. Along toward evening when they were in slightly better country Nolan led westerly through a thin stand of pines to a small meadow with a creek bisecting it.

They had jerky. If they'd had more it wouldn't have been cookable because they had no fry pan. Nolan surprised Ash. He led his horse to the creek and washed its back. He hobbled it out there and returned to drop down in the grass. "Where you from, Mister Whatever-your-name-is?"

"Fitzhugh. Ash Fitzhugh. I'm from a lot of places. Lastly New Messico." He told Nolan about the map which would take him to Montana, and Nolan laughed. "Too cold up there anyway, Mister Fitzhugh. In the cattle business if you spend all summer puttin' up feed to get you through the winter, you'll never get rich."

Ash looked askance at Nolan. "You don't have hard winters in Idaho?"

"It gets cold enough here to freeze the buzzoms off a flat-chested woman.

But the mountains provide protection. It's not paradise but it's better'n what I've seen of both Montana an' New Messico. One stays cold too long, the other's got a short grazin' season." Nolan gazed out where the horses were grazing. "I got somethin' for you to think about. I need three riders. Come gatherin' and markin' time I hire on two more temporary." Nolan paused to look at Ash. "I got to hire three men when we get to town. I need a rangeboss. I done it for damned near thirty years an' that's long enough . . . you interested?"

Ash made a crooked small smile. Nolan'd made him this offer before. A lot of things were different then. He said, "I'll ponder on it," and rolled out his bedding, kicked out of his boots, coiled and rolled his shellbelt and holstered Colt within easy reach.

He remained awake for an hour or so. The only sound was Nolan snoring. If he took up the offer he'd be able to keep an eye on the old man who, strictly speaking, was not his obligation except that he liked the old gaffer, and since Lisa and Caleb would leave . . . He fell asleep.

The following day they struck out in the dark. Nolan wanted to reach town before dark. As it had been the day before they rarely spoke even when they stopped to water the horses.

Ash had known men like Fred Nolan, quite a few in fact; it seemed very successful stockmen had the same traits, even in some cases the identical characters. Those were the cowmen who worked hard. There was never enough good land. Those other men had used the same tactics to enlarge their land holdings which meant driving off homesteaders, stump ranchers and many others who tried to squat on land they had used for many years.

Nolan also had a mean streak, and that was not unusual either. If there was something Nolan had which not many stockmen had, it had to be his ability to look a six-gun muzzle in the eye without showing fear.

They broke camp in cold darkness, were on the trail long after moon-set which meant they could rarely make good time, the trail was too treacherous in the dark.

Ash was accustomed to going long periods without eating and evidently the short man in the lead was also like that.

They passed rocky ground and eventually, with the sun turning red on its descent, entered a wide area with encircling distant mountains. Nolan twisted to point and say, "Wildroot."

As they approached Ash studied the town. It had long buildings from a generation earlier. It resembled a scattering of houses, like bees, hovering around a very large two-storey structure with a high peaked roof. Its log walls were hoary and it had a covered porch all along the front. There were saddle and wagon animals out front along the tie racks.

Nolan did not twist again when he

said, "One side is the store, the other side is the saloon."

Dusk was settling when they entered Wildroot from the south. It seemed to be a quiet place, which most towns were during supper time.

The liveryman was also a freighter. As he often said, liverying in an isolated place like Wildroot was a starve-out business. He was a large, thick man with a full beard and small pale eyes that peered from beneath bushy brows. When they turned in to have their animals cared for the liveryman addressed Nolan in a rumbling deep voice. "Good evenin' to you, Mister Nolan. I'll take 'em." The liveryman reached for both sets of reins with a hand the size of a small ham. When he looked enquiringly at Ash, Nolan introduced them. "This here is Ash Fitzhugh, my foreman. Ash, this here is Max Schultz."

They shook hands before the massive bear of a man led two tired horses down his barn runway.

Nolan threw Ash an ironic look. "In Wildroot it's best if someone knows you. They don't like strangers."

Across the wide roadway and south of the general store and saloon was a café squeezed between two larger log buildings. Nolan was also known there. The caféman was a potbellied fifty-five year old. He greeted them wearing a clean apron over a dirty shirt.

Except for Nolan and Ash the eatery was empty. The caféman explained about this in a loud voice from his cooking area. "Four fellers stopped the Deadwood – Wildroot stage in the hills north-east this morning. Got off with Mister Featherstone's money box. Folks went after 'em but them lads had a good four-hour start."

When the meal arrived Ash did not hesitate. He had learned long ago that while hunger can be put off, when its owner eventually eats, he doesn't stop until every pleat is out of his insides.

Nolan and the caféman talked. Ash ignored them. Nolan had also to be hungry but he ate slower so he could talk. It seemed that Rex Featherstone, the emporium's proprietor, had sent north his bullion box which was to be returned from a bank up there so Featherstone would have more ready cash.

The caféman said whoever robbed the coach had to know which stage to stop and where it would be, coming south. Nolan added a suggestion. "It'd be fellers from close by who knew about when Rex would send out for money and when it would get back."

The caféman sucked his teeth in thought before nodding. "More'n likely. Old Featherstone's fit to be tied. He's harpin' on Wildroot hirin' a fulltime lawman again."

When Nolan led off in the direction of the largest building in town, the balding older man, wearing black sleeve protectors, left a clerk to handle a customer, came over and spoke without a greeting. "Sons of bitches stopped the coach with my money box on it."

Nolan answered calmly. "So I heard," saw the suspicious gaze Featherstone put on the stranger accompanying Nolan, and introduced Ash, again, as his foreman.

They passed into the darker saloon, which only had one window and it was small. The result was that briefly morning sunlight brightened the place.

Nolan introduced Ash to the barman, a thin individual with coal-black hair which he parted in the middle. He also wore black sleeve protectors, and something else, a diamond stickpin big enough to choke a chicken. Nolan nodded toward a shelf with six individual bottles on it, one for each of the saloonman's biggest cowmen in the territory.

As the barman poured into a pair of jolt glasses he dryly said, "I expect Mister Featherstone told you about highwaymen gettin' his money box."

Nolan nodded, downed his drink and pushed the glass aside. Something Ash would learn about Nolan was that he rarely drank. The barman eyed Ash askance — stranger. Ash smiled and toyed with the little glass.

The barman said, "I expect now we'll get a lawman. We will if Mister Featherstone has anything to do with it. He's been around all day madder'n a wet hen."

The barman didn't smile. In fact he never smiled. His problem was that he'd been raised Southern Baptist; they called liquor 'the devil's brew'. If the barman could hire out anywhere else in Wildroot he'd shed his apron in a minute. One thing was in his favour: he never preached of the evils of drink, but every time he watched someone down a jolt, his frustration increased a smidgin.

Nolan took Ash across to the saddle and harness works. The proprietor wiped both hands on his apron and greeted Nolan like an old friend, which in a way he was. Nolan had commissioned him to make a saddle to Nolan's specifications. That had been last winter. The harnessman said he had the tree bullhide covered and was fixing to cut the swell covering and the skirts.

Nolan's gaze never left the saddler's face. He introduced Ash again as his foreman and after they had shaken hands Nolan said, "Mister Nailor, when I was young I apprenticed out to a saddle an' harness maker. We turned out good saddles in one month."

The saddlemaker, who had heard the stories about Fred Nolan, pushed up a weak smile. "It'd have been done months back, but I had to go down south to my cousin's funeral. You know how it is, Mister Nolan, one damned interruption after another."

Nolan said, "Did you ever hear that excuses are good only to them as make them?"

The saddlemaker fumbled below his counter, brought out a beautifully engraved pair of sterling silver conchos and put them in front of Nolan as he said, "You ever seen workmanship like that?"

Nolan and Ash leaned to admire the conchos. Ash wanted to smile, as a means of changing the subject it would probably have worked on nine out of ten men, but Fred Nolan was one of the ten.

The saddler smiled broadly. "I can let you have them both for two dollars."

Nolan straightened up. "How much longer before I get the saddle?"

The saddler's smile withered. "Three weeks?"

"I'll be back in three weeks. For your sake I sure hope it's finished."

After they left the saddler's shop Ash looked back. There was no light showing from the front window. Nolan stopped on the plankwalk where there was an overhang roof. The town showed many lights. Nolan went to a bench and sat down. Ash did the same. Nolan said, "I like Wildroot. Someday when I retire I'd like to move down here."

Ash had also liked the town. It

was a functional relic of days when it had been a freighter's rendezvous to haul away hundreds of stiff, salt-cured buffalo hides. Many places like Wildroot had become ghost towns unless there was a railroad. Wildroot was many miles from the tracks and seemed to do very well in spite of that.

Nolan was gazing across the road at the emporium when he said, "You ever stop a stage?"

Ash answered dryly. "Never did."

Nolan surprised his companion when he said, "I did. Rode with the Jennings brothers. Their speciality was trains. I never liked that. They got shotgun guards whenever the trains were carrying valuables."

Ash had heard of the Jennings brothers. There were two of them, both short men. The youngest was a redheaded man who would fight a buzz saw at the drop of a hat.

Nolan turned his head. "That's where I got my start. Saved every dollar so's I

120

could quit outlawin' an' get set up in the cow business."

Ash nodded. "You got set up right well, I expect."

"Yes, but I've had to fight for every damned acre I run cattle over."

Ash tipped back his hat. "Includin' old man Wolff?"

For a moment the short man hung fire before speaking, and when he did what he said brought Ash straight up on the bench.

"Last summer I went down to New Messico to buy bulls. You know New Messico, do you?"

"I've been there."

Nolan made a tight, humourless smile. "I expect you have. They had a picture of you posted out front of the general store."

Nolan gave Ash a steady look then changed the subject. "There's advantages to bein' in Idaho, damned few towns got marshals. A man could live out his years an' never run into anyone who'd seen wanted dodgers

121

nailed on the front of general stores."
Nolan paused. "A foreman in Idaho
workin' for a big outfit might grow a
beard, but it wouldn't be necessary. I
told you what I'd pay."

Ash shoved out his legs and slumped
against the bench. The evening was
beginning to get cold. He did not
say a word for so long a time that
Nolan slapped his legs and stood up.
"The roomin'-house is that run-down
building at the north end of town. I'd
say we've earned a sleep."

Ash did not move as he regarded
the short man. "How much reward
was there?"

"Three hundred dollars. If a man's
only worth three hundred dollars, I'd
guess what he done wasn't real bad."

Ash slowly arose. "You want to hear
about it?"

Nolan shook his head. "Let's see if
the old witch who owns the boardin'-
house has a couple of rooms."

When they reached the dilapidated
porch, Nolan said, "I hope it wasn't

horse stealin' because you're ridin' a horse wearin' my brand." Nolan showed that tough small smile again. "Figured I'd mention it if you got a notion to leave in the night."

7

The Trail Back

IN the morning on their way to the greasy spoon Ash was quiet and Nolan, who ordinarily was not talkative, stopped outside to face the taller and younger man. "Forget it, Mister Fitzhugh. I have."

Ash was also quiet during breakfast, the only one of the caféman's customers who was. There were townsmen, stockmen, some freighters and a few strangers. Mostly, the talk was about the highwaymen who made off with Mister Featherstone's money box. There was considerable snide humour. Featherstone was a brusque and well-off man and folks just naturally enjoyed it when something like that happened to well-off people.

Outside the sun was rising ponderously.

It gave off brilliant light but precious little warmth.

Nolan took Ash back to the saloon where there was a side wall where notes were pinned. Out of a dozen or so rangemen seeking work Nolan selected three names, returned to the bar and asked the long-suffering Baptist if he knew any of those three.

The barman knew them all. Nolan asked his opinion of them and the barman said just one, a buckaroo named Barry Ohlund might not be what Mister Nolan was looking for. Ohlund was the son of a *pistolero* down in southern New Mexico who had been leader of a band of Mex *bandoleros* notorious for robbing banks, stealing cattle and horses, and shooting up towns.

Nolan went back to the note board, picked out another name and returned. The barman watched him do this and when Nolan mentioned the name Frank Horton, the barman nodded in the direction of some card players. One was redheaded. "That's him," the barman said, "He's worked for most of the outfits hereabouts. I expect he'd be rated a top hand."

Nolan left Ash at the bar to interrupt the card game and ask if the redheaded man wanted work. He did. Nolan hired him on the spot and gave a cryptic order. "Me'n my foreman'll meet you at the livery barn in an hour." When Nolan returned to the bar the card players spoke softly and hurriedly. Frank Horton was unimpressed. He said, "Cash me out. I know who he is. I've heard his reputation." As he arose he also said, "If it don't work out, well, I was lookin' for work when he hired me."

The other two riders were loafing at the blacksmith shop. One was grey, lined and weathered. He said he was George Hess. He also said he'd hire on. The other rangeman was little more than a boy. His name was Randy Huffington. When Nolan hesitated the older rangeman said, "He'll get the job done, Mister Nolan. Take my word for it."

Nolan told them pretty much what he'd told Frank Horton. He had some business to do at the savings bank and for Ash to be down at the livery barn when the new hands appeared.

Ash had seen no sign of a bank for an excellent reason. The local banker owned and operated a freight line. His office — and massively impressive big steel safe — were in his freight office.

Nolan had no difficulty. Even if most of the money in the safe hadn't been his he wouldn't have had. The freight-line owner got the money, counted it, had Nolan count it; then, as they shook hands the freighter did something he should have known better than to do. "That's a heap of money, Mister Nolan. You fixin' to buy something, are you?" Nolan's cold gaze made the other man instantly aware of his breach of frontier manners. He was red as a beet as Fred Nolan left the office, crossed the large palisaded freight yard and headed for the livery barn. The sun was now high enough for the day to be pleasantly warm.

The waiting men arose from the bench outside the livery barn as Nolan arrived. There were five rigged out animals dozing at the tie rack. Two of them wore the Nolan brand.

They had got so late a start Ash anticipated two, instead of one, dry camps after nightfall.

Randy Huffington dug out a harmonica and demonstrated his uncommon ability with the thing.

Nolan did not push the horses. He too was reconciled to perhaps two overnight camps. When Ash rode stirrup with him Nolan looked around. "I got Wolff's money. I expect his girl an' Caleb'll be leavin'. Like the old man figured, bein' far off from anywhere ain't no life for the young. How old are you, Mister Fitzhugh?"

That kind of directness did not sit well with westerners. Ash said, "Thirty-four. How old are you?"

Nolan answered without hesitation. "Sixty-seven. Old enough to be your pa."

Ash rode along questioning that possibility and forgot about it when they found a good place to water and rest the stock.

As they sprawled in shade the red-headed man said, "This here is pretty much up-ended country."

Nolan jerked his head in Ash's direction. "He thought he was in Montana." The three new hands laughed. Ash didn't but he smiled.

When they struck out and had ridden enough miles to be comfortable with each other, the youngest rider jacked up his nerve and asked Mister Nolan where his ranch was and how big it was.

"We'll make it by tomorrow night," the cowman stated. "I figure the range is about seven miles west an' a little north — clear of the broke-up country." Nolan looked at the youth. "You range rode before?"

It was the weathered, faded man, George Hess, who answered. "He's been with me four years, Mister Nolan. We've worked for big outfits an' we run wild horses in Messico. That's where he learned ropin'."

Nolan stopped, leaned on the saddle swell and regarded the older man and the youth. He told Hess the lad was old enough to answer a question without a spokesman, and an unsmiling George Hess said, "He's my nephew. His ma was my sister. Her'n his pa died in a border-jumper raid at a place called San Gracia close to the border. They burnt the town an' killed everyone they didn't take away with 'em back into Messico." Hess's pale gaze was fixed on Fred Nolan. "He can do as good as I can an' I been hirin' out twenty years an' more. Mister Nolan, keep out of the lad's private life. He's beginnin' to get over it. Bringin' up the past don't help."

Ash saw colour mounting in Nolan's face and broke the silence between the pair of older men when he said, "It's a long way, we can talk on the trail."

The clash between Nolan and Hess ensured a long ride in silence. The new riders were particularly careful to avoid anything unpleasant.

Ash rode up with Nolan where the trail permitted. After a while he said, "You could have done it different," and Nolan turned on him. "All I done was ask the lad a question," which was true. "How was I to know Hess was his uncle an' all the rest of it?"

Ash's reply was succinct. "Well, now you know."

The tension lasted until dusk when they left the trail to reach one of those postage stamp meadows with a creek that Nolan knew about.

They ate jerky, drank creek water, and the ones that smoked lighted up. Ash didn't smoke. He made a sortie to make sure the horses were safe and the redheaded rider named Frank Horton walked out too. He rolled a smoke in silence, a sure indication he had

131

something to say, and after lighting up he said it. "I need work, but I ain't sure I want to work for Mister Nolan."

Ash's reply was quietly given. "He's tough an' hard. If you do the job you'll never have nothin' to worry about."

"But the way he butted into that young feller's business . . ."

"He didn't know the lad's story or he wouldn't have, but he's a blunt man."

"George Hess didn't like it," Horton said.

"Neither did I, but Hess settled the business. Mister Nolan'll be careful."

"How long you been his foreman?"

Ash reached up to scratch the side of his nose before answering. "You done the same thing; askin' personal questions."

Horton shifted his feet. "It ain't the same as Mister Hess did."

"It might be, Frank, if I was as touchy as Hess is, which I'm not. Ride along, look the place over an' if you don't want to stay that's your business."

Ash watched Horton walking back to his blankets and blew out a quiet breath. How long had he worked for Mister Nolan? He didn't work for him — not now and maybe never.

Nolan was impatient so the following morning they were on the trail a few hours after moon-set, Nolan out front because he knew the way, the others strung out like ducks following their mother.

They stopped once, only a few miles from the ranch. It was close to the arroyo where Ash had caught Bill Jones. That was not mentioned, in fact the way Nolan acted that event might not have occurred nor the fierce little war following. It helped that when Nolan up-ended his canteen George Hess tossed his over and Nolan drank, tossed it back and said, "Much obliged."

The tension vanished. It turned out that Frank Horton hid a puckish sense of humour behind his ordinarily solemn expression. He told jokes and some colourful lies, and when they were ready to bed down the five men were relaxed in one another's company.

Nolan used a stick and dazzling starshine to draw a dust map which approximated to the size and location of his holdings and Randy asked how many cattle Nolan ran and got an honest answer. "I'm not sure but last spring we tallied and marked an' the gate count was nine hunnert cows with one bull to each forty cows."

Randy's curiosity was up. When he glanced at his uncle, Hess almost imperceptibly wagged his head. It was innocent prying that had started the earlier feud. The lad settled under his blankets with a saddle-seat for a pillow and eventually the older man bedded down.

The following morning Nolan was in a hurry. By his calculations they should have his yard in sight before high noon.

A couple of hours into the new day

Frank Horton said, "I smell smoke. We must be gettin' close."

Nolan abruptly heeled his horse over into a lope leaving the others. When the new men would have followed Ash held out his arm after which they poked along until there was a dip then a rise. Nolan was sitting up there like he was carved of rock. The others halted. Ash tipped down his hat against newday light as he said, "Was there someone at the house when we rode out?"

Nolan's reply was waspish. "There wasn't no one. You see smoke risin?"

"Yes."

"That stove pipe is out of my kitchen at the main house."

"Then you got visitors." Ash innocently said and Nolan turned on him. "I don't get visitors," after which Ash kept silent.

The smoke rose straight up because there was not a breath of air stirring. They sat on the rise for the better part of half an hour before Nolan said, "Whoever it is got no business

being there. In my house, damn it."
He looked at Ash. "Would that be old
man Wolff?"

Ash doubted it very much. "No.
Why would he be down there?"

Nolan lifted his rein hand. "I'm goin'
to find out. No, not that way, follow
me." He led them westerly through
country that was wicked on horses
and did not stop for a breather until
they rode atop a knoll where trees hid
them.

Fred Nolan's expression was murderous
as he led westerly off the knoll, picked
his way to country where the plinths
and aeons-warped spiky hill ridges fell
away to a country only Nolan among
them had seen before. His miles-deep
grazing territory. They followed him
like sheep, even Ash had no idea
where they were going. He'd never
seen Nolan's cow country before.

By the time they were able to skirt
along southerly in country horses could
handle without effort, the sun had
passed overhead. Ash thought it was

about mid-afternoon but that didn't bother him. Ash was one of those men who could sense trouble. He could sense it now as he rode behind Nolan until the cowman abruptly halted, and they all halted.

They were about a mile or such a matter from visible buildings. There was no longer smoke showing, and as much as they could see of the yard nothing moved.

Nolan picked his way south-westerly to the rim of a deep arroyo, slid his horse to the bottom and waited until the others had done the same amid clouds of pale dust and loose earth.

They followed the arroyo for close to a mile before Nolan stopped, handed Ash his reins, climbed to the rim and while lying belly-down up there considered his yard. If there had been movement he was now close enough to see it. There was no movement.

He slid back down, dusted off, got astride and led off again. No one spoke.

Clearly Fred Nolan was in no mood for conversation.

Where the arroyo tipped upwards it was no longer possible to be hidden from sight but they were slightly less than half a mile from the yard and the way Nolan led them, with his huge log barn to shield them from detection, they came out of the arroyo and loped, minimizing at least their period of exposure.

As they thundered toward the rear of the barn a man suddenly appeared, roused no doubt by that many loping horses.

He was framed in the wide barn opening for seconds. They saw him clearly. He was young and wore the customary shellbelt and holstered Colt but he also had a six-gun in the front of his britches.

Seconds later he was out of sight.

Nolan flung off his animal racing for the barn. Ash wanted to shout a warning. It would not have made any difference, Nolan was fighting mad.

The three riders with Ash veered toward a corral where they tied their animals. Except for Ash the others were wary and cautious.

Inside, the gunshots were thunderous, four in rapid succession. Ash swore and led off with the others following, guns in hand. Ash hugged the log wall and eased toward the opening. He removed his hat and squatted before peeking inside.

There were two men sprawled and motionless. One of them was Fred Nolan. Ash turned to George Hess. "Mind the house. Nolan's been shot."

As Hess led the others away Ash entered the barn, gun cocked and ready, but the heavily armed man must have been the only interloper in the barn, and he was dead without having a chance to use his holstered weapon. He had two wounds both in the chest. Either one would have ended his life.

Fred Nolan was face down and inert. When Ash knelt to roll him face up,

Nolan said, "Did I get the son of a bitch?"

Ash nodded as he looked for wounds. There was only one and it was in the right side. The bullet that had knocked Nolan down had ploughed a gash where it had entered and exited; Nolan was bleeding copiously.

A man shouted from the direction of the main house. Ash paid no heed. He went to the dead man, who had dropped a pair of saddle-bags to run out back. Ash dumped both pockets on the ground. He picked up a pair of recently washed longjohns and a clean but faded and wrinkled shirt and went back.

He was satisfied people did not die from the kind of wound Nolan had, provided the bleeding could be stopped and, afterward, they got no infection.

While he was concentrating on staunching the flow of blood and wrapping someone's long-johns tightly around the cowman, shots were exchanged between the house and the new hired hands who seemed to have taken cover on both sides of the yard among outbuildings. As Ash worked and listened, he decided the new hands were a long way from being greenhorns.

Whoever was forted up in the house seemed to have plenty of ammunition. The new hands were more selective, they seemed to fire only when there was a target.

Nolan growled past clenched teeth. "Leave me be! Go lend a hand outside!"

Ash rocked back on his heels regarding the older man. "If he had been a better shot he'd have — "

"Gawddammit, go lend a hand!"

Ash stood up as he said, "I'm goin', Mister Nolan. You sure can be a cranky old bastard can't you?"

There was no response but the cowman's gaze did not leave Ash's back until he had disappeared around the south side of the barn's rear wall.

Gunfire was now down to an

occasional shot as Ash felt his way carefully to the south-west corner of the barn. There was a log well house closer to the main house and between it and the barn. Ash took down a breath and sprinted. He could only have been seen from the house if whoever was in there went to a room at the extreme west end, and evidently no one had done that because Ash reached the well house safely, heart pumping like a trip hammer.

Someone yelled from across the yard in the vicinity of the three-sided smithy. "Your friend in the barn is dead. Keep this up an' so'll you be. You ready to quit?"

The answer was three shots, one of which struck the anvil and whined across the yard.

The man who had called did so again, his voice as unperturbed as it had been before. "All right, you stupid sons of bitches." The yell was followed by a fusillade of shots one of which shattered the only glass window in the front wall, and for a time afterwards the forted-up men did not return the fire, they had been too busy ducking and hiding.

From the shooting across the yard Ash figured there were two men over there. He had no idea where the third man was until someone emptied a six-gun into a door at the back of the house.

That had clearly been a signal. The men in the vicinity of the smithy cut loose again. They'd had plenty of time to reload.

As they fired Ash moved to the edge of the well house and emptied his handgun too. It sounded like a war for several minutes before the men across the yard paused to reload, then fired as furiously as before. Whoever was in the house had no chance to get close enough to the broken window to fire back.

From the corner of his eye Ash saw a long-legged man racing toward the house firing as he ran. He held his breath. It was the new rider named Frank Horton. He did not duck toward either corner but bounded up the steps to the porch where he flattened to shuck out spent loads and plug in fresh ones from his shellbelt. He then leaned as far as he dared and emptied the handgun through the window.

Inside someone shouted desperately. "That's enough Gawddammit! That's enough!"

Horton called from the porch. "Come out, hands on top of your heads. *Now!*"

The man inside called back. "I'm comin'. Don't shoot."

Ash heard the man try to open the door which had been hit by several bullets close enough to its edge to have jammed it.

The man tried to use both hands. It was no use; he had to give up the attempt. Horton shoved his six-gun in front of him as he pushed on the door. "You and your friends come out."

The captive answered hoarsely, "They can't. See for yourself."

Ash crossed to the porch, and young Randy Huffington and George Hess appeared from the vicinity of the smithy.

Frank Horton shoved the door aside and stepped into the doorway. Mister Nolan's parlour was a shambles. Two men were dead, one sprawled in a chair, the other over by the stone fireplace. The third man was sitting with both hands to his face. One sleeve dripped scarlet and one boot was unnaturally twisted.

Horton jerked his head for Ash to join him. They entered the parlour and Ash was astonished at the degree of destruction. Even some old portraits on the south wall had been riddled.

He leaned briefly over the pair of dead men before going over to face the man with his hands to his face. He gently tapped the man's shoulder. "Lower your arm." The man obeyed without looking up. The arm had been broken below the elbow. The man had to be in pain but when he finally raised his head all Ash saw was an expression of shock so deep the man probably could not feel pain, but he would shortly.

Mister Nolan was yelling like a lobo wolf from the barn. Ash sent George Hess and the youngest among them to fetch Mister Nolan to the house.

He and Frank Horton went rummaging for something to set a broken arm with and came up with the top off a cigar box.

As they worked the wounded man would not look at either of them, even when they hurt him. He locked his jaws and sat there. They were finishing with the splinting and bandaging when George Hess and Randy Huffington eased through the doorway with Fred Nolan on a blanket.

The cowman looked up and around and fell back. Ash jerked his head for Huffington and Hess to find a bedroom and put Nolan there.

As they passed the man with the bandaged arm Nolan raised his head. He glared without saying a word. The wounded man would not meet his gaze.

8

Nolan's Foreman

THEY hauled the dead men out to the porch for the time being, fed the wounded man whiskey and while waiting for it to take effect set upturned chairs and benches the way they should be, and ignored Nolan's growls and groans.

The wounded man said his name was Arthur Crampton. He said the man who had been sent to the barn to rig out horses had been Sam Cotter. Almost indifferently he identified the pair of corpses on the porch as Wright Barbour and James Colton.

Ash pulled a bench up close and asked what the four of them had been doing in Fred Nolan's house, and Crampton's reply made everyone in the room stand stock still. "We was on our way out of the country after stoppin' a stage north of Wildroot. We seen this place from the hills an' come to get fresh horses. We should have got 'em an' gone on, but every one of us was dog tired."

Crampton raised brown eyes with muddy whites. "An' you fellers come before we could get away."

Ash had a question for Crampton. "What did you get off the coach?"

"A money box full of greenbacks."

"How'd you know there was a money box on the stage?"

"We didn't." For the first time Crampton showed interest. "We was on our way south from Montana, hopin' to reach Messico, when we seen the dust an' set up an ambush. Mister, luck was with us."

From over by the door George Hess said, "It's your kind of luck that fills cemeteries," and headed for the barn.

He returned fifteen minutes later with a pair of saddle-bags slung over his shoulder. Without a word he dumped them at Ash's feet, then stood waiting impassively. Ash unbuckled both sides, raised the flaps and stopped dead still. The bags were full of greenbacks. Crampton said, "That's it. Sam took it with him, this set an' his personal saddle-bags." Crampton's face clouded. "Son of a bitch!" he exclaimed and did not say another word.

George Hess called from the porch. "Rider comin'."

Ash stepped outside, watched briefly then started toward the barn. He did not have to wait long; Caleb Wolff came into the yard slowly and cautiously. Even after he recognized Ash at the tie rack he studied the house, the yard, the entire area from narrowed eyes. When he reached the barn and leaned to swing down he said, "Sounded like a damned war. I was out pot huntin'."

Ash leaned on the hitching pole. He was dog tired and the day was many hours from being over. He explained to the old man's bearded, burly son what had happened. He also told Caleb how it had happened, and Caleb did not take his eyes off Fitzhugh, not even when Frank Horton and George Hess began dragging the dead outlaws toward the barn by the heels. Eventually he asked a question. "Mister Nolan . . . ?"

"In the house nursin' a wound in the side along the ribs."

"Didn't get killed, then?"

"No."

Caleb scratched. "These strangers . . . ?"

"He hired 'em to replace the others who left."

Caleb loosened slightly. "You'n him went to Wildroot?"

Ash made a thin smile. "An' brought back the money."

Caleb lightly slapped a leg with the tag end of his reins. Ash made a guess about why he had done that and said, "As soon as he can be up an' around I expect he'll come over."

Caleb considered the reins in his hand. "Might be quite a spell, wouldn't you say?"

"Might be. He bled out pretty good."

"Well . . . supposin' Pa come over here."

Ash nodded." Fine."

"Ash . . . ?"

"Yeh."

"About yourself. Pa said after all you done for us, we owe you."

"Forget it, Caleb. If things were reversed you'n your pa would have done as much for me."

"Pa told me'n Lisa last night we'd got to make it right with you."

Ash straightened up off the hitch pole. "You folks don't owe me, an' I'd take it kindly if this kind of talk ended right here." To soften his words, Ash smiled. "We're friends, Caleb, an' it's likely we will be for a long time."

Caleb gazed steadily at Ash for a long moment before saying, "What does that mean?"

"Mister Nolan wants to hire me on as his rangeboss."

"Are you goin' to do it?"

"Maybe. Most likely. If I do, Mister Nolan'n me got to have an understandin' about you folks an' any others he's been bullyin'."

Caleb pulled the reins through his fingers a couple of times before nodding and, turning to get astride, said, "I'll tell Pa to come over for the money."

As Ash watched Caleb ride away George Hess came from the barn to say, "He don't seem like a friendly cuss."

"He's got reasons," Ash said and started in the direction of the main house.

When he entered the bedroom he was shocked and angered. The bandaging he had improvised was soaked with blood. He kicked a chair around to sit, then remained standing as he said. "You damned fool! You want to bleed to death? Gawddammit you're more trouble than a herd of monkeys! Turn toward me an' don't say a damned word. *Turn!*"

Nolan turned. Ash began removing the soggy bandage. When he was finished and straightened up he said,

153

"Don't move," and left the room to search for fresh bandaging. Randy and the wounded outlaw were talking. As Ash passed on his way back to the bedroom he glanced at them. Crampton seemed to be trying to sleep. Ash told the youth to go down to the barn and help his uncle.

When Ash entered the bedroom Nolan hadn't moved but he'd had time to recover from being blessed-out. As soon as Ash went to work cleaning the wound, Nolan said, "I don't think I want you for a foreman after all. No one talks to me like you done."

Ash finished the cleansing and began the rebandaging as he replied, "I wouldn't hire on with you for ten times the pay. You're a disagreeable, mean son of a bitch. *Quit moving!* What you done to old man Wolff . . . you should've been hung. From what I guess he's not the only one. Mister Nolan, quit your gawddamned squirming. It's got to be that tight to hold the hide together. *Hold still!*"

Nolan did not move. His face was red as a beet; if anyone had ever unloaded on him like Ash had done, it must have been many years ago.

When their eyes met Nolan's shone fury. Ash's gaze was steady and unwavering. "Old man Wolff's comin' over for his money."

"How do you know he is?"

"Because Caleb rode in a while back. I told him to have the old man come over. It'll be weeks before you can ride over there. You got any objections?"

Nolan appeared to be biting back words. "You don't say what's goin' to be done on this ranch."

Ash dried soggy hands and arms, flung the soggy cloth aside and sank down on the chair, he was tired to the bone, and exasperated. He and Nolan locked stares. When Ash spoke he sounded tired. "I've known my share of cowmen like you. Miserable, overbearin', domineerin' sons of bitches."

"By Gawd, if I was able I'd stomp

the waddin' out of you. I almost done it — "

"But you didn't. Lie still, I'll fetch some medicine."

This time Ash's search required more time, but eventually he found the whiskey and returned to the bedroom with it. Nolan scowled. "You drink it, I never liked the stuff."

Ash said, "Neither did I, but open your mouth or I'll straddle you an' pour it down."

Nolan opened his mouth, swallowed three times and raised a hand to dash away the tears. After exhaling several flammable breaths he said, "Did you try any of old man Wolff's homemade whiskey? It goes down smooth as molasses. This stuff is pure poison."

Ash stoppered the bottle and put it on the lamp table beside the bed. He did not say whether he'd tasted old man Wolff's liquor or not. Instead, he said, "We got to bury the dead ones an' do somethin' with the other one."

"Hang the bastard," Nolan exclaimed.

Ash gazed at the short man who looked even smaller in the bed. "I don't think so," he said quietly, and Nolan's flushed face turned quickly. "There's no law in Idaho except maybe in one or two towns. Folks been buryin' outlaws here since before I come into the country. Keep the son of a bitch until I'm up an' around. I want to lean on the rope."

Ash blew out a breath of resignation. "He's got a busted arm an' an ankle he can't put no weight on, an' he told us what we wanted to know . . . An' he's — "

"You missed your callin', Mister Fitzhugh. You should have been a Bible banger."

Ash picked up the bottle, considered it briefly then tipped and swallowed twice after which he fiercely grimaced, and Fred Nolan laughed.

George Hess appeared in the doorway. "Six riders comin' from the south," he announced, and left the doorway.

157

Nolan started to push upwards. Ash arose, put a hand on his chest and said, "Lie back. If they want to see you I'll bring 'em along. You don't move in that damned bed."

As Ash raised up Nolan eyed him with a fierce stare. "You bring 'em to me no matter who they are."

Ash met the grizzled and greying rider named Hess in the parlour where Hess said, "They're armed to the gills. I recognized a couple of 'em. Fellers from Wildroot."

Ash went out to the porch, watched the riders a moment then walked with George Hess across the yard to the barn tie rack where they waited. Hess's nephew and Frank Horton had been watching the oncoming horsemen. Hess told them to get farther back in the barn and keep quiet.

When the riders were nearing the yard George Hess suddenly exclaimed, "That's Mister Featherstone; the feller with the gut, ridin' the eleven-hundred-pound *grulla*."

Ash nodded, yanked loose the tie-down thong over his holstered Colt and when the riders entered the yard and the portly storekeeper raised his right hand, palm forward, Ash returned the salute.

Featherstone dismounted like a man who had been absorbing punishment, sprung his knees a couple of times as his companions also dismounted and said, "Fitzhugh, isn't it? Glad to see you, Mister Fitzhugh. Is Mister Nolan around?"

One of the townsmen with Featherstone led his animal over into shade and abruptly squawked. He hadn't seen the lad and Horton, they were out of sight, but the three dead men lying side by side in the middle of the barn runway were visible to anyone close enough to look inside.

The startled rider said, "Three corpses in there!"

George Hess and Ash Fitzhugh did not move as the Wildroot riders crowded in the doorless front opening of the barn. From behind them Ash said, "We got your money at the house, Mister Featherstone. There was four of 'em. You're lookin' at three, the other one's over at the house."

Featherstone turned. "They was the ones that robbed the stage?"

Ash nodded. "And headed south, stopped here because no one was around for food and fresh horses. We come in behind 'em. Three dead, one alive." Ash jerked his head and Featherstone followed him in the direction of the main house.

Featherstone's companions got their second surprise when Horton and young Huffington appeared out of barn gloom.

George Hess, who had remained behind when Ash and the storekeeper crossed toward the main house, laughed. No one else did.

The moment Ash opened and closed the front door Nolan yelled at him. He ignored it, handed Featherstone the saddle-bags and watched his expression

160

change as he sat down to count the money. He even ignored the ragged individual rubbing sleep from his eyes with one hand. Nolan yelled again, swearing this time.

Featherstone paid no heed until he was satisfied with his currency count, then he looked up and Fitzhugh jerked his head.

They appeared in the bedroom doorway where Nolan glowered. "Got your damned money back, Rex?"

Featherstone put on his most grateful and unctuous smile. "All's there, Mister Nolan. Good thing they rode south ain't it?"

Nolan's glare widened. "Good thing?"

"Well, I mean about the money." Featherstone went to the chair at bedside and sat down. It was the first thing he had sat on for a couple of days that wasn't moving. "You're lookin' fit," he told Nolan, and got a frosty reply. "I always look fit when some son of a bitch shoots me."

"That feller in the parlour — he was one of 'em?"

"Yes."

"Well," stated the storekeeper getting to his feet. "We'll take him off your hands, take him back to town an' have a public hangin'."

Ash spoke before Nolan could. "We'll keep him here, Mister Featherstone."

"Here? Whatever for? Oh, you gents want to hang him. Well, for a fact it seems you got first choice. Well, gents, I'd like to head back while there's still daylight. I don't like to leave the store with the clerk any longer'n I have to."

As Featherstone turned to leave the bedroom Ash asked him a question. "It's a long ride from Wildroot to here. Did you figure them outlaws would be hereabouts?"

"Well no," the storekeeper replied. "Not exactly. Riders from town went up where the stage was stopped and figured to track from there . . . You know Charley Wing?"

As Ash shook his head, Nolan spoke

162

from the bed. "In'ian."

Featherstone smiled toward Nolan. "Trapper, hunter, lives north of town. He seen the coach get stopped. He come to town an' told me the highwaymen went south."

As Featherstone nodded and left the bedroom, Nolan said, "He come on horseback?"

"Yes, with a posse. Why?"

"In all the years I've known him I never saw him on a horse." Nolan looked steadily at the younger man. "Why'd you say we'd keep that outlaw here?"

"You can't guess?"

"No."

"Maybe someday I'll tell you."

Ash was in the doorway before Nolan spoke again. "You can't change the spots on a leopard."

Ash agreed. "Likely you can't, but turnin' him over to old possum-belly and his town riders, with a busted arm and bad ankle, don't set well with me neither."

Ash returned to the yard as Featherstone and his companions were getting to horse. He exchanged nods with them and went into the barn before they had left the yard.

George Hess, Frank Horton and Randy Huffington were waiting. Frank said, "It's gettin' warm," and nodded in the direction of the three dead outlaws.

Ash nodded. "Get some diggin' tools, I'll get a wagon."

As the sun sank it should have gotten cooler but not this day, and where they dug three graves there was no shade. Randy brought a canteen from the wagon to pass around. It was during one of these periods of rest that greying George Hess mopped off sweat and asked Ash about the fourth outlaw. He got no response for a long time, not until they were back digging again, then all Ash said was, "I know what you're thinkin', but it goes against my grain to hand over a bled-out man with a cracked elbow and a bad ankle."

Whether the others accepted that or

not nothing more was said.

It had been one of those days whose peril and uncertainties drained men without them realizing it until supper time, then they sat loose and mostly quiet. They ate but without the customary appetite of rangemen, and when the three hired riders headed for the vacated bunkhouse to bed down, Ash got two lamps set close by and examined Crampton's injuries. The ankle was swollen to about the size of a small flour sack. There was no way Crampton could get his boot back on. The arm throbbed. Ash fed the outlaw. Neither of them spoke until Ash helped Crampton to a leather sofa and got a blanket, then, as they looked at each other Ash said, "I'll leave a saddled horse on the north side of the wagon shed."

Crampton considered Fitzhugh for a long time before saying, "Thanks."

"Wait until late. It's goin' to be hard walkin'."

"I'll make it."

Ash nodded and went down to the bunkhouse where the hired rangemen were sleeping like the dead.

He slept the same way. The horse he'd left north of the wagon shed was also sleeping, but while the two-legged creatures did not awaken until after sunrise the horse awakened hours earlier, stood like a rock while a handicapped individual the horse had never seen before gritted its teeth as it struggled to get astride, evened up the reins and kneed the horse into a quiet walk. It was cold and the man had no coat. He rode seven miles eastward before halting to lean over the saddle. He'd been hurt before, many times, but nothing had ever caused the variety of pain his swollen ankle caused.

When he nudged the horse into moving again he told it through clenched teeth that as long as he lived he would never stop another coach, steal another horse nor rob another store.

The horse plodded on loose reins,

indifferent to the sounds of its rider. Most rangemen talked to their mounts.

When sunrise came the rider saw a few lights of a town southward and kept on riding. He had no idea how far he had come nor what kind of country he was passing through. All he knew was that he had to keep riding until there was so much distance between himself and that ranch back yonder that while they could certainly track him, they would be unable to overtake him even though they might lope and he had to walk because he would not stop until the following night, and even then for not very long.

It wasn't every day a man escaped being lynched. Nor was it every day that, sick and sore, he made decisions that would guide him for the rest of his life.

Why that tall man back yonder the others called Ash had done what he had done was something the outlaw would wonder about the rest of his life — and never find the answer to.

9

Discord

GEORGE HESS stood a long time gazing at the ground. The outlaw hadn't saddled and bridled the missing horse. In fact judging from droppings the horse had stood in one place most of the night.

Frank Horton came up, looked at the sign and said, "He never rigged out that horse. Lookathere; one bare foot one booted foot. George . . . ?"

Hess turned an expressionless face to Fred Horton. "He's gone. That's all I know," and walked out back to lean on a corral where Fitzhugh eventually joined him. Hess did not say a word until he'd squinted skyward. "If we're goin' to do any ridin', it's goin' to be on a cold trail." Horton gazed at Fitzhugh.

Ash nodded. "We got other things to do." He jutted his jaw in the direction of three approaching riders. "Visitors; you gents hang and rattle. When they tie up tell 'em to come to the main house."

Hess watched Ash cross toward the house, lifted his hat, vigorously scratched, reset the hat and walked up through the barn. His nephew and Frank Horton were already out front.

When old man Wolff, his son and daughter dismounted, Hess told them to go to the main house, he'd take care of their animals. Randy stared at the girl until his uncle nudged him to take the reins.

Mister Nolan had spent a good night. He had a fading headache and when Ash appeared in the doorway to say the Wolffs were in the yard, Nolan used a sleeve to dry watering eyes. He ignored the announcement to ask about the outlaw.

Ash answered showing no expression.

"He stole a horse an' escaped in the night."

Nolan hung fire before speaking again. "From what I saw he couldn't have got outside to pee."

"Mister Nolan, you never had to make a choice between gettin' hung or crawlin' like a dog not to."

Old man Wolff called from the parlour. Ash went to meet him and lead the way to Nolan's bedroom. All but Caleb Wolff showed shock at Nolan's appearance. The old man went to the bedside and said, "There's a doctor up in — "

"Eighty miles from here, Mister Wolff. By the time he got here I'd be up'n around or dead."

Wolff blew out a breath and sat on the chair at the bedside. "Caleb said you got shot."

Nolan's impatience surfaced. "Your money's in a paper sack under my pillow. I expect you'll sign a quit claim."

Wolff nodded making no move to

reach beneath the pillow. "There's somethin' that might help until you can be up'n around, Mister Nolan."

"Is there?" Nolan replied sourly.

"Lisa here is as good a nurse as they have in towns for man or beast."

Nolan's eyes went to the girl briefly then back to the old man. "I'm gettin' along fine, Mister Wolff."

"She'll stay with you for a spell anyway," the old man said and faced his daughter. "All right with you, Daughter?"

"Yes Pa." Lisa met the hostile gaze from the man in the bed.

Nolan started to make an angry statement when Ash, who had been leaning in the doorway, spoke first.

"I'd take her up on it, Mister Nolan."

"An' who in hell asked you, anyway?"

"No one," Ash replied. "But the kind of nursin' you need comes best from a woman."

"You been doin' just fine," Nolan exclaimed and Ash's retort almost stopped the cowman's breathing. "I won't be around."

When Nolan recovered he spoke in a rising tone of voice. "Twice rangeboss pay an' all you got to do is boss things?"

Ash turned and went from the doorway to the parlour where he crossed to the porch and went down across the yard in the direction of the barn.

The silence in the bedroom was deep and lasting. Caleb found a chair and offered it to his sister but Lisa remained standing so Caleb sat. They watched Nolan in silence. He stared a long time at the empty doorway before starting to swear and Caleb came up off the chair. "Mind your mouth, Mister Nolan. There's a lady present."

Nolan barely acknowledged the menacing appearance of the young Wolff. He looked at the old man. "After all I done for him."

Caleb spoke again. "Liked to have

172

got him shot. I'd say he don't owe you any more'n I do."

The old man stood up. "She'll need a private bedroom."

Nolan glared at the old man until Lisa approached the bed then shifted his gaze to her. Lisa said, "Can I see where you got shot?"

Nolan yanked the covers up under his chin with both hands. "Not on your life, young lady."

Lisa smiled and said, "Caleb . . . ?"

As the burly, bearded man approached the bed Nolan yelled at the old man. "Get 'em away from me!"

The old man saw the whiskey bottle, ignored the others to pick it up and swallow, just once. As he put it down he looked for something to spit in, found nothing suitable and swallowed, after which he told Nolan the whiskey was the worst dregs he'd ever tasted, to which the cowman made no reply as Caleb leaned, gripped the blankets and pulled them down, despite Nolan's best effort to prevent that from happening. When their faces were close Nolan addressed Caleb through clenched teeth.

"I'll kill you."

Caleb nodded, got the blankets down and straightened up as his sister and the old man leaned close. Lisa said, "He needs disinfectant, Pa," and raised her eyes to Nolan. "You got some?"

"Horse liniment," Nolan spat at her, and Lisa again addressed her father. "You or Cal could fetch the medicine box."

The old man spoke to his son. "Go fetch it, son."

"I'm not goin' to leave you two with this — "

"*Go fetch it, son!*"

Caleb stamped out of the house, encountered the rangemen and Ash Fitzhugh in the barn, brushed past them to get his horse and George Hess, who had been jostled, said, "You'd ought to mind your manners, furry-face."

Caleb, already furious, came around

with a snarl and lunged, Hess yielded ground until he was beyond reach of the ham-sized fists, shook his head and quietly said, "You overgrown son of a bitch," and feinted Caleb, who lunged again both fists high. Hess hit him squarely on the point of the jaw, Caleb did not even gasp. He went down in a heap and George Hess went out back to soak his right hand in the water trough.

When he returned Frank and Ash had Caleb on his feet. He was clear-minded but unsteady as he watched Hess come in from out back.

Hess smiled without a shred of humour. "Mind your manners, furry-face. Next time I'll put you down for all time."

What impressed Ash was that at no time had George Hess showed anger.

They watched Caleb rig his horse and without a glance at them ride out of the yard. He stopped halfway home to lean and spit a trickle of blood and gingerly feel a loosened tooth.

No one ever told Fred Nolan of this incident but if they had it might have done a lot toward raising the cowman's spirit.

Lisa examined the wound, showed none of her revulsion and sat on the bedside chair to tell Mister Nolan what he needed was stitches, but without them as tightly as someone had tied the torn flesh it would eventually heal and leave an impressive scar.

He asked if she had ever done anything like this before. She had, on horses and cattle, many times, but only once before on a person, and that had been when her brother was mauled by a bear.

Old man Wolff told Nolan, Caleb had minor scars, and as Nolan would have reached under the pillow Lisa caught his arm and stopped all movement. "Don't raise your arms over your head," she told the cowman. "And don't try to get up or bend. It's goin' to take quite a spell for that wound to heal."

Nolan looked straight at the girl. "I got a cow outfit to work, young lady."

"You have a rangeboss, Mister Nolan."

"You heard what he said!"

"I'll talk to him," Lisa replied and arose to leave the room. Neither the cowman nor her father said anything to detain her but after she was gone Nolan said, "He's a hard-headed man, Mister Wolff. Ain't no girl alive that'll influence him."

The old man sat down gazing at the whiskey bottle. "You'd ought to know better'n buy saloon whiskey." He said this reproachfully. "Anybody who'd drink that horse piss can't be a real whiskey-sippin' individual." Old man Wolff then said, "You know how to write?"

"Yes."

"Well then, since I don't you'll have to write up that quit claim . . . Just one thing you got to put in it — "

"I know; that you can live over there

as long as you want."

Old man Wolff smiled. "You're a pretty savvy individual, for a mean, trouble-makin' son of a bitch, Mister Nolan."

"Mister Wolff, I don't want that girl on the place!"

"You got her, Mister Nolan, an' let me tell you somethin'; I've only known two women in my lifetime who had real medicine hands. Her ma an' Lisa. Somethin' else. Be decent to her because her brother don't like you one bit."

It was late afternoon before Caleb returned. There was no one in the barn when he led his animal inside to be off-saddled, stalled and forked a manger full of feed.

As he was leaving the barn young Randy came around from the corrals and nodded. Caleb eyed the youth, grudgingly returned the nod and went to the house.

Old man Wolff was asleep in a parlour chair. Caleb roused him, handed him the medicine box and asked where Lisa was. The old man did not know. He took the medicine box and went to the bedroom, from there he called for Caleb to find his sister and bring her to the house.

Fred Nolan eyed the box as the old man put it down and reached for the bedside chair. Nolan said, "Horse medicine?"

"An' for busted-up humans." The old man leaned forward. "Give her a chance. What the hell, you can't be no worse off."

"I might not be no better off neither."

Wolff threw up his hands. "You're just naturally a pig-headed, disagreeable bastard. Folks offer help, an' you cuss at 'em."

"Why should you want to help me?" Nolan asked.

Old man Wolff thought before replying. "No good reason, bein's it's you, except that me'n my brood take care of hurt things. We just naturally do. I was raised like that an' I raised my boy'n girl the same way." The old man eased back in the chair. "But for a blessed fact I can't explain even to myself why we'd do you any favours — you cow-stealin', horse-poisonin', bushwhacking miserable bastard."

Nolan's face did not get red as he stared at the older man. Whatever he might have said was blocked by the appearance of Lisa in the doorway. She went to the medicine box, put it on the bedside table and as she opened it she said, "This will most likely smart, Mister Nolan."

The cowman growled his response. "Do what you got to do."

Lisa sent her father to fetch a bowl of hot water, leaned to peel away the bandage with Nolan's eyes never leaving her face. He said, "Why ain't you married, girl?"

She went on working as though she had heard nothing, but when she eventually straightened up she said,

180

"Why aren't you married, Mister Nolan?"

From the doorway Lisa's father, holding the basin with both hands, said, "Because the good Lord wouldn't do that to any woman."

Nothing more was said as Lisa cleansed the wound and peppered it with white powder shaken from a regulation salt shaker. It stung but Nolan would have died before he showed anything.

This time the bandage was a roll of cloth from the medicine box, and when Lisa cinched it tight that also caused pain, and as before Nolan's eyes never left her face nor showed pain.

When she finished Lisa rinsed both hands in the basin and smiled at Nolan. "We'll do that every day for a spell, until it's scabbin' over. Mister Nolan, you need an all-over bath."

That remark got action. Nolan glared, pulled the covers up as he'd done before and snarled. "You keep out of this room unless I call for you, an' there'll be no washin' of body parts!"

Lisa cocked her head a little. "I'll send Mister Fitzhugh an' some of the riders to bathe you."

Nolan's gaze widened. "He's still here?"

"Who?"

"You know who! Fitzhugh."

"He's out with the other men. When he comes back I'll send him to see you."

Lisa left the room with the basin, her father followed along. At the doorway he turned, winked at Fred Nolan and said, "You missed out a lot, Mister Nolan. Don't never underestimate the way female women do things."

By nightfall only the old dog who lived under the porch was in the middle of the yard, his destination, which had been the bunkhouse where he always chummed men out of food, had been interrupted by a vigorous set-to of scratching.

Over the years his successful forays had been worthwhile. When it rained water stood on his back.

Coyotes howled from the northwest and two cranky horses engaged in a snorting and snapping contest. Otherwise the night was quiet.

Fred Nolan could not sleep. He blamed it on inactivity, which it could have been. It could just as easily have been the kind of bleak thoughts a lifelong, hardshell bachelor had when, as with other things in life, his convictions turned out to be incorrect. He had dedicated his life to his cow outfit. There had been no time for women. In fact Nolan disliked women, not because he had formed that dislike from association, because he had not known that many women, but simply because . . . He swore under his breath and eventually slept.

Lisa brought his breakfast on a tray. He'd never eaten in bed in his life. She helped prop him up, put the tray on his lap and said, "Mister Fitzhugh'll be along when you're finished."

He let her reach the door before

saying, "You'n him talked? Never mind. Who rassled this meat, it ain't cooked plumb through."

She said, "Eat it anyway. And mind, don't spill the coffee."

She was gone before he could retort, and for a fact he was hungry. It caused pain when he extended one arm so he managed with the other arm, and though the meat was not cooked plumb through, it was close enough.

When he finished he put the tray beside the medicine box on the bedside table, leaned gingerly back and sighed. For fifty damned years, or close to it, he'd run his outfit from the saddle and all of a damned sudden he was being swamped with folks he did not like, except for Fitzhugh, and come right down to it he was beginning to dislike him too, not just because of the way he talked back, but because no man in his right mind would refuse to work for someone who would pay him twice what he was most likely worth.

He was sawing logs when Lisa came

for the tray, and did not hear her tell someone in the parlour Nolan was sleeping, and that if he would come back in an hour or so.

The following morning Caleb rode over, stalled and fed his animal and was crossing toward the main house when a man called from the corral to lend a hand at earing down a horse while his eye was doctored. Caleb changed course, did not see the man needing help until he was at the corral. They exchanged a look when George Hess said, "Both ears, Mister Wolff."

Caleb climbed through the stringers, got hold of the frightened horse and set back. Hess picked a splinter from the eye and sprayed it from a shaken bottle. "Ease up," he said and Caleb freed the horse which immediately raced to the far side of the corral and shook its head.

George Hess said, "Much obliged."

Caleb eyed the older man for a moment before nodding. "Any time, Mister Hess."

10

The Ruse

LISA watched until she saw Ash leaving the bunkhouse on his way to the barn, and hurried after him. Ash stopped and turned. "I thought about it last night," he told her.

She swiftly said, "You can't go back on your word!"

Ash's gaze drifted away then back as he nodded. "All right, but like I told you leopards don't change their spots."

They crossed to the porch where she stopped and looked up. "The things we talked about — "

"I know, I thought on 'em. He's goin' to be laid up a spell, an' given enough time he'll have to accept changes. But, Lisa, like I told you, I never liked bullyin'."

She opened the door, waited for him to enter first then remained in the parlour to watch him walk toward the hallway leading to Nolan's bedroom, then she got busy in the kitchen.

Nolan, who had been staring at the ceiling, lowered his eyes as Ash came through the doorway and said, "That girl's quite a woman."

Ash occupied the bedside chair and tipped his hat as he nodded — and waited.

Nolan cleared his throat. "This here," he told the younger man, "is sort of like eatin' crow."

Again Ash nodded, expressionless and silent.

Nolan's temper rose a notch. "You ain't makin' it any easier."

This time Ash spoke. "I figured on things a long time last night, Mister Nolan, an' agreed with Lisa that I'd talk to you in the mornin', but the longer I figured the less I come to think you'n I could ever really hitch horses."

Nolan made a quiet statement. "Did you know the law talked to that feller who drew you the map on how to reach Montana?"

Ash's eyes widened. "No. Where'd you hear that?"

"I didn't hear it but I know lawmen. They'd trail you to that place the feller drew the map for you."

Ash frowned. "You're blowin' smoke, Mister Nolan."

"There's a chance I am, an' an even better chance I ain't. But what I'm sayin', Ash, is that if they're trailin' you they'll go up to Montana. They won't find you there because you're in Idaho. In fact you're about as far south in Idaho as a man can get, with no towns worth the name, no lawmen, an' a job runnin' FN cow outfit for as long as you like."

Ash removed his hat, held it in both hands between his knees and studied it a long time, during which Fred Nolan said nothing.

When Ash finally spoke he was blunt.

"You'n me are as different as night from day. Things you've done to build your cow outfit I wouldn't do. You got a nasty disposition. I expect that more'n anything else would make us lock horns sooner or later." Ash raised his eyes to the man in the bed. "It just wouldn't work, Mister Nolan. I know — I told Lisa I'd try'n work at it. It'd be a waste of time for both of us. You want a rangeboss, hire Caleb Wolff."

Nolan's eyes popped. "He hates my guts an' has for years."

"Well, that new rider, George Hess, would make you a good rangeboss. He's got the savvy an' the experience."

Nolan's tongue made a snake-like circuit of his lips. He said, "So far we've talked about things that could happen, not about what will, or even might, happen."

Ash looked puzzled. "What's that mean?"

"Hire on as rangeboss for three months. After that if it ain't workin',"

Nolan shrugged, "no hard feelings if you ride on."

Ash heard someone in the parlour. He arose, considered the older man for a moment then said, "Three months."

Nolan waited until Ash had departed then reached under the covers to vigorously scratch. While he was doing this Lisa appeared in the doorway, and gasped, "Don't do that," she exclaimed and came to bedside. "It'll itch for a fact, but don't scratch. Let it scab over."

He removed the hand from beneath the covers and said, "Sit down."

She took the bedside chair.

"He'll stay for three months. After that . . . " Nolan shrugged.

Lisa considered the hands in her lap. "Don't let him leave, Mister Nolan."

The cowman's gaze went to the girl's face and remained there. Instinct told him what was happening. Except for instinct, since he'd had no experience with female women, he would not have had an inkling.

Lisa said, "I'll fetch you something to eat."

He watched her leave the room, puffed out his cheeks and expelled a long breath. With all his other problems, for Chris'sake, he now had this one without the faintest idea what to do about it, or what to say. He wondered if old man Wolff suspected his daughter was sweet on Nolan's foreman. Probably not, old Willford Wolff and Fred Nolan had *that* in common.

Ash, George, his nephew and Frank Horton rode out. Ash had no idea where FN's boundaries were and did not ride out seeking them. He had been a stockman all his life, except for one unfortunate interlude, and riding with men who had the same background they looked for, and found, bunches of FN cattle.

They also found water-holes and two places where cattle as well as wild animals, spent hours licking rock slabs as slick as grease. Salt licks were not uncommon. It was always a good idea to know their locations. It made riding on a gather much simpler knowing those things.

They returned just ahead of settling dusk, cared for their animals and trooped to the bunkhouse. There was a mostly depleted bottle of popskull and while they were shedding spurs, guns, shellbelts and hats Caleb Wolff walked in with an earthenware jug which he placed on the table, and departed.

Frank Horton made a dry comment. "That feller reminds me of a bear with a sore behind." The jug went around and was sampled again by men whose revived spirits and expanding compassion decided that Caleb Wolff was a feller after a rangeman's heart. Wherever he got that remedy for aches and pains, it had been crafted by a gen-u-wine still man.

George Hess only allowed his nephew some in a cup which was two-thirds full of water. Randy downed it like it was all water, stood a moment gazing in the direction of his bunk, took three steps in that direction and fell flat.

The other men owlishly eyed him before George lifted Randy, pushed him to the bunk, flattened him there, removed his shellbelt and boots and turned to see Frank and Ash looking steadily at him. George said, "It was two-thirds water."

No one questioned that statement. Even if they'd wanted to someone banging on the door would have prevented it.

Ash opened the door, glimpsed Lisa at the same time he was distracted by the sound of running horses. Lisa said, "I saw him. It was too dark but it was a man an' he deliberately opened the gate and stampeded the horses."

Ash, George and Horton followed her to the empty corral with its sagging-open gate. She said, "I came down to grain the stalled ones. I saw a shadow pass in front of the rear opening, moving careful. He went to the gate, lifted it as he opened it so it wouldn't drag, and waved his hat to run them off."

Ash told Frank to go west, George to go east, while he would go north. He was not hopeful. The night-rider would have had a horse tied or hobbled nearby.

But none of them heard a running horse, and that bothered Ash until George dryly said. "He led the critter at a walk before he got astraddle."

They returned to the bunkhouse where Lisa saw young Randy flat out on his bunk, sleeping. She looked at George. "Is he sick?"

"No ma'am. He's just plumb wore out. We covered a lot of country today."

She went to the door. "I'd better tell Mister Nolan," she said, and closed the door leaving three rangemen standing as solemn as owls. Ash eventually sank down eyeing the jug without making a move to touch it. Frank Horton put all their thoughts into a statement when he said. "What'n hell for?"

George suggested what had been his first idea. "Damned horse thief."

Frank scowled. "There's horses all over the range, George. Sneakin' into a yard . . . Hell; he could have got himself killed."

Ash went out to the small porch where the air was crisp and chilly. That was how raiders operated; run off the horses so's folks was afoot, then come in the night with guns and torches. But to his knowledge raider bands had been hunted to extinction years back.

He considered lights at the main house. Lisa would have told Mister Nolan. Ash could imagine the old cowman's reaction.

George Hess came out to roll and light a smoke. While trickling a bluish-grey banner upwards he said, "I expect Mister Nolan's got his share of enemies."

Ash agreed. "For a fact, but runnin' off our usin' stock won't amount to more'n a little trouble gettin' 'em back.

He missed the ones stalled in the barn."

George studied the pinpricks of light above. "He either didn't know that or . . . ."

"Or?"

"Ash, there's somethin' wrong here. I can't put my thumb on it. Don't make sense to just run off the using horses for spite. That's takin' too big a risk to make some inconvenience."

George stamped his quirly to death, gazed pensively in the direction of the lighted main house and shook his head. "Just a hunch. I've had 'em before that didn't amount to a hill of beans. I'm goin' to bed down."

Ash remained outside. Hess's words had made him feel uncomfortably restless. He strolled to the barn, went down through to examine the empty corral and the open gate, and ended up leaning on some pole stringers musing.

Eventually, he followed Hess's example and bedded down. There was little that could be done before daylight, then go find the using stock and bring it back. And next time use a chain and padlock on the gate.

Nolan sent Lisa to fetch Ash to the house. When he entered the bedroom Nolan said, "Who was he? Or was there more'n one?"

Ash was annoyed, he and the hired riders had been in process of saddling up at the barn to go manhunting and also to bring back the using horses. "I don't know a damned thing more'n you know, Mister Nolan. I'll let you know what we find out when we get back."

The sun was halfway above the horizon when the riders left the yard. Lisa watched them. Her brother was with them. Her father had gone back home the previous evening. She'd thought Caleb had gone with him, and maybe he had. Caleb had always been an early riser. Whatever the reason for him being at the Nolan place so early, she could see him riding with the others.

It was one of those mornings when the sky was flawless blue, visibility was excellent and warmth would eventually arrive.

Excepting Caleb none of the riders had more than a cursory knowledge of Nolan's range, but finding loose stock did not require a whole lot of knowledge, horses travelling fast in a bunch left tracks a blind man could follow.

What Ash wanted was the sign of a rider, or several riders veering away from the loose stock. He found no such sign.

George Hess watched tracks, scowling. When Caleb came up Hess said, "Something's wrong. Whoever spooked the horses would be crazy to ride with 'em. Once he'd got 'em scattered good he should go in a different way."

Caleb said nothing, but he also began to look worried, and eventually when they halted atop a landswell to look for horses Caleb told Ash it was beginning to look to him as though the night-rider was still with the using horses and, if that was true, why then it seemed to Caleb that the son of a bitch was a horsethief, not just someone acting out of spite against Mister Nolan.

Randy resolved that issue by standing in his stirrups and pointing to a distant small band of grazing horses.

They left the landswell and loped until they could distinguish individual animals when it became clear this band consisted of the using horses they had been searching for.

As they loped Caleb told Ash either he was wrong about a horsethief being responsible, or likely the horsethief, and friends if he had some, being compelled to let the horses 'blow', were up there somewhere lying in ambush.

Ash held an arm aloft after which they rode at a walk. Beyond the grazing animals was a stand of blowsy old cottonwoods where a skinny warmwater creek ran. Except for those trees there was no cover.

George Hess told his nephew to stay

with the others and began a slow-loping ride southward. As the others watched Hess began to close his large circle which would put him on the far, or west, side of the grazing horses.

Frank Horton muttered, "Damn fool. He's a sittin' duck."

But no gunfire erupted.

Before starting the drive back with the recovered animals Ash led the others in a search. They did not even find horse tracks leading away from the using stock, and that was a genuine puzzler.

The recovered livestock had run hard last night. Moreover, these were not mustangs, they were accustomed to riders and to being eased southeasterly in the direction of Nolan's yard.

There was no need for haste, it was a beautiful day, their mission had been accomplished and if they'd hurried it still would be close to dusk before they reached the home place.

They stopped twice to loosen cinches and let the horses graze. Each time they did this the loose stock fanned out to also graze.

The men remained puzzled. Caleb told George Hess it made no sense unless whoever had run off the using stock did it to annoy Mister Nolan, and Hess thought that was possible. From what he'd heard in the Wildroot country Mister Nolan had precious few friends and a passel of enemies.

Frank Horton, chewing a grass stem while lying in tree shade at their last stop, wagged his head. "What bothers me is what become of the son of a bitch. Even for spite he should have left off as soon as he stampeded the horses, then gone home."

Ash, who knew the countryside better than all but Caleb, said there was no place the night-rider could go home to. Unless he rode one hell of a distance, because there were only two places in the area, the Nolan place and old man Wolff's place.

Caleb shook his head. He had arisen before sunrise and had arrived in the

Nolan yard while it had still been dark, and he neither saw nor heard anything that could have been a rider.

It was a puzzler and it accompanied the men when they got the loose stock heading in the right direction again. The sun was blood red in the west, teetering close to some distant sharp pointed peaks.

By this time of day the using horses knew their destination and dogged along at a steady walk.

When they reached the yard the only light shone from the main house and the old dog did not bark, which did not necessarily have a significance, he had been having difficulty hearing for the past year or so.

After they had cared for their animals and chained the corral gate closed, someone fired a pistol inside the house.

For several seconds no one moved, then Ash led off in a race to the porch, six-gun in hand. What he saw when he burst inside stopped him dead in his tracks, Fred Nolan was lying in the middle of the parlour floor and there was blood everywhere. He was conscious. They took him to the bedroom where Ash held a lamp close. The wound was still bleeding; he told Caleb to fetch Lisa. Caleb returned after a thorough search to say he could not find her.

They got some whiskey down Nolan, who choked and gagged, but it seemed to help. He said he had been firing the six-gun at long intervals and had been down to his last bullet when the horse-hunters had burst into the house.

Caleb shouldered the others roughly aside and leaned as he said, "Where is my sister?"

Nolan was sweaty. "He took her with him."

"Who took her?"

"Rider who quit, name of Jones." Nolan needed another pull on the bottle, dashed water from his eyes with a blood-flecked sleeve and spoke again, in a firmer voice. "He come to the house an hour or so after you fellers went horse-hunting."

Ash sought the chair and sat down. He and George Hess exchanged an understanding glance. The horses had been run off last night to ensure the riders would go after them come morning, which is exactly what they had done.

Nolan said, "I tried to fight. It wasn't no use. He mopped up the floor with me, got the six thousand dollars, took Lisa, and left."

Caleb said, "Which way did he go?"

Nolan had no idea, he had passed out after crawling on his hands and knees to the parlour for a gun to signal for help with.

Frank Horton took a pull on the bottle and slumped against the wall as he said, "Too dark now."

The others nodded, except Caleb who said, "If I got to feel the tracks on foot I'm goin' to find that son of a bitch."

Ash was considering Fred Nolan when he said, "Saddle me a fresh horse, Caleb. I'll be along as soon as I make a new patch for Mister Nolan."

They left Ash alone with Nolan. Ash was rough because he hurried, and when he replaced the soggy bandage with a fresh one he said. "Did he know the money was here?"

Nolan answered through clenched teeth. "He knew. Don't ask me how, but he knew." Nolan paused to hold his breath from pain before also saying, "All the time he worked for me I never figured him to have a clever notion, but he sure did this time — drew you fellers out after the loose stock, then all he had to deal with was me an' Lisa." Nolan finally could not repress the groan and as Ash settled him on his back the cowman said, "I didn't think he'd still be in the country. Sure as hell he heard down at Wildroot I'd taken a sizeable bunch of money out of the safe. Things like that just plain get talked around, specially in a place no bigger'n Wildroot."

As Ash dried his hands on the discarded bandage and turned to leave Nolan said, "Crowd him. Don't let him stop or sure as hell it'll be bad for the girl. Crowd the son of a bitch for all you're worth."

Ash hesitated in the doorway. Nolan looked like a warmed over corpse. He said, "Maybe old man Wolff'll show up."

Nolan nodded. "Maybe. Remember — crowd him."

It was excellent advice for daylight — but even with a sizeable moon it would be impossible unless the pursuers knew in which direction the renegade was travelling and even then it would not be possible to race ahead if he headed northward through the broken hills and peaks in the direction of Wildroot, which Ash did not believe he would do.

Nor did he. Caleb walked ahead on foot leading his animal. Once having determined which way a pair of fresh tracks went, he followed the sign in a bent-over hike, mindless of riders behind him.

Jones, or whatever his name really was, was making tracks in a south-westerly direction. The man needed to trade space for time and the only direction in which he could do that was to head for open country where no hills or rough areas would slow him.

Nolan's riders had been a-horseback since before sunrise, they had every right to be tired, hungry and saddle-weary and perhaps under different circumstances they would have been, but aside from Caleb Wolff's blood-thirst, none of the others would have stopped to rest if their lives had depended on it.

When they eventually had rolling to flat country ahead they could not push the pursuit because the tracks of two horses, while faintly discernible, could not be relied upon not to alter course. They man-hunted slowly but inexorably.

Ash told George Hess he did not

believe the renegade would stop, and as the moon sank lower it became clear Jones would not stop.

The predawn chill was scarcely noticed and the only time Caleb spoke was when he came across scraps of discarded food. He growled something the others had difficulty understanding but it had to do with making Jones look like a piece of meat when he found him.

Dawn came slowly. Full daylight did not arrive for another hour or so, but when visibility definitely improved Caleb got into the saddle and boosted his horse over into a lope.

What bothered Ash was that, with excellent visibility in open country they did not see a pair of riders. Frank Horton thought Jones might have gone to ground, might have holed up somewhere, but the country they were passing over offered no evidence that there could be such places.

Eventually Ash called a halt to rest the animals. Caleb handed his reins to

Randy Huffington and coursed ahead on foot. George watched him go and wagged his head. "If he finds the son of a bitch," he said, "by the time we catch up there'll be nuts, guts and feathers scattered all over hell."

11

Ino

THE toughest men on the ruggedest horses had a limit, and by mid-afternoon it was being reached for both. The horses plodded along head-hung, their riders alternated between exhausted little catnaps, and weary postures in their saddle with no conversation. Only Caleb did not appear to be wearing down. He kept his horse at a fast walk, was no less than a quarter-mile ahead when he abruptly halted. They could see the way he was sitting perfectly erect.

As they approached Caleb twisted in the saddle, called something, and sat forward, both hands atop the saddle horn.

A mile or so ahead there was what

appeared to be either a soddy or a square building of adobe. It had trees around a vast, barren-looking yard, a set of scrub brush corrals, too low for cattle or horses, and where a rope had been stretched between the corners of two buildings, someone's laundry limply hung.

Hess asked Caleb who lived yonder and Caleb shook his head. He had never been this far south-east before. He'd never had reason to be.

Caleb made a sweeping gesture of open country in all directions. There were no trees other than the ones by the house, and precious little undergrowth. What there was an abundance of was grass; it ran on for miles.

Caleb eased his horse ahead. The others followed. When they were closer they made out a dray wagon beside the house and a high faggot corral for animals larger than sheep and goats.

The corral was empty and there appeared no sign of life until the man-hunting riders were close enough for a light grey and white dog to appear, hair up along his neck, barring the rider's advance by standing stiff-legged and challengingly. Ash and Caleb were riding stirrup when they halted. Caleb drew his six-gun without haste and raised it. Ash's descending arm knocked the gun from Caleb's hand. As Caleb dismounted to retrieve the weapon the goat-eyed dog made a half-hearted rush. Caleb swung back into the saddle glaring at Ash, who said, "He's doin' what he's supposed to do."

Caleb growled his reply. "You go roust 'em out then."

Ash handed the reins to Caleb, swung to the ground and walked directly at the dog, who yielded but not until the last minute when a man's voice called roughly and the dog slunk away.

The man in front of the mud house had a double-barrelled scattergun in the bend of one arm. He was not as old as Ash and while his clothing was clean it was also bordering on being ragged.

He did not smile when he greeted Ash. "Evenin', mister. Somethin' I can do for you?"

Ash nodded. "A man an' a woman ridin' together. Accordin' to the tracks they come this way."

The man with the shotgun replied. "They did. We sold 'em some milk'n cheese, grained their animals and got paid well for it." The man shifted his shotgun. "Is there somethin' wrong?"

George Hess dryly said, "Six thousand dollars worth of wrong, friend, an' the young woman bein' taken along as a hostage."

A woman appeared behind the man in the doorway; she was young, but squatter women aged fast. She said, "Jake, I told you."

The man did not look around. "After they left my wife said the woman was being took along against her will."

Ash nodded without allowing the conversation to get any further afield. He asked if the man and woman had said anything he remembered, and the homesteader shook his head. "Didn't talk much at all. Like I said, we fed 'em, grained their animals, and the man give me a five dollar bill." The settler held up the greenback, clearly enormously impressed that he had been paid five dollars for nothing more than some grain, cheese, and hard bread.

Frank Horton went around back and returned pointing northerly. Caleb growled at Ash and the settler. "Much obliged," he told the settler. To Ash he said, "We're losin' time."

The settler looked squarely at Caleb when he said, "Mister, you keep pushin' those horses an' you're goin' to end up on foot."

Without a word George Hess dismounted, tugged the latigo loose, asked where the trough was and led his horse to it. Caleb was the last to favour his mount. When the settler went rummaging in a shack for grain Caleb dropped his reins and picked up tracks of two horses and did as he'd done the previous night, followed the sign like a hunting dog.

The settler said, "Got a bee under his blanket?"

Ash replied shortly. "The woman is his sister. The man who made her go with him is a renegade."

The settler accepted that rebuff calmly. "Well, goin' north like he done when he left here is goin' to take him close to a place called Ino. It's where we get supplies, about six, eight miles north. He's goin' to need fresh horses an' supplies." When they eventually took up the trail on refreshed animals the settler waved and watched. His woman came out to stand beside him.

It was easier to track Caleb whose imprints were fresh, and when they finally saw him, every one of them was surprised. George Hess said, "Must have trotted."

Caleb must have done something. He was standing on a sod bluff close to three miles from the settler's place.

When they came up Frank Horton handed over the reins of Caleb's horse he had led and Caleb toed in, swung up and evened his reins with his back to others as he said, "I know that place. Years back when we had horses I come over this far once." As he led off he also said, "Ain't much more'n a well an' a peach tree at the side of the road."

When they were close enough to make out details Caleb's description seemed to fit. Ino's outstanding feature was trees, not just the usual pines and cottonwoods but fruit trees, which lent the place a pleasant, hospitable look. Ash reined easterly and dismounted as he said, "Frank should scout ahead, the others might be recognized." Caleb seemed not to have heard. As Frank Horton rode away Caleb said, "If they're down there I want that renegade to myself."

No one commented.

It was warm, the day was wearing along and the horses were glad for a rest. They picked grass, switched tails at deer flies, and when the men sat down the animals provided shade.

George Hess squinted at his nephew, and smiled. Randy smiled back. Hess said, "It ain't always lookin' at the butt of a cow . . . If there's trouble you duck and keep out of it."

The lad brushed a hand over the old holstered Colt. "I practised," he said, and Hess nodded, said no more, lay back in the grass with his hat over his face and slept.

Frank returned with the sun sinking lower off in the west. He dismounted, fished in his saddle-bags and handed out cheese, bread and salt crackers. "The store's where life exists, otherwise it's mostly older folks with chickens and fruit trees."

Caleb chewed cheese as he said, "Did they stop there?"

Frank was eating a peach when he nodded. "Stopped there to buy fresh horses. There ain't but a handful of horses down there an' they ain't for sale."

Caleb swallowed and glared. "You're awful damned calm."

Frank nodded looking directly at Caleb. "Got reason to be. Feller at the store put 'em up in a shack out back until Jones can go among the cow outfits to find horses."

Caleb topped chewing. "You mean they are down there?"

"Yes," Frank replied ruefully eyeing peach juice on his shirt. When he spoke again he addressed Caleb. "My guess is that he won't take your sister with him when he goes horse-huntin'. He likely figures he's too far ahead to worry about us."

Ash gazed in the direction of the village, a sleepy, shady place that time and progress had forgotten. He'd seen places like Ino before, many of them, and had occasionally thought that someday he'd like to settle in such a place.

Caleb yanked him out of his reverie when he arose saying, "I'm goin' down there!"

George unwound up out of the grass, thumbs hooked in his gunbelt. "No you're not! You're goin' to wait until dark like the rest of us. *Set down, Caleb!*"

Caleb did not sit back down but neither did he move out of his tracks as he and Hess stared at each other. Ash said, "Caleb, this ain't just your war. We'll go down there together."

Caleb did not move, neither did the man who had whipped him days back. Frank Horton broke the tension. "We can lie in wait until Jones goes horse-huntin'. Then get your sister. It'll be better'n bustin' down there now, start a fight an' maybe get her hurt."

Caleb reluctantly sat back down in the grass. So did George Hess. When next he addressed Caleb his tone was softer. "I got an idea that son of a bitch lacks a lot of bein' a greenhorn. We're likely to get just one good chance to get your sister out of the way. After that, if you want to gut the bastard I'll loan you my knife."

If this had been intended to assuage Caleb the bearded, burly man gave no indication that it had succeeded, but when Hess offered part of the gnawed block of cheese Caleb accepted it and very gradually made an almost imperceptible nod of his head.

Ash walked out a ways to study the settlement. Daylight was fading when he returned, tossed his hat aside and sat down. Caleb abruptly said, "Suppose he steals horses tonight in the village and runs for it?"

Frank Horton had the answer to that. "I wondered about that an' nosed around. There's no more'n six or eight horses down there an' they're mostly as old as I am an' splay-footed from scratching in garden plots."

Their horses had filled up and were standing hip shot, replete and drowsy.

Ash watched the sun disappear, strolled back to watch for lights and when he saw several he returned to say they could bed down for a spell, they had plenty of time, and asked

Frank if he had seen the shack the storekeeper had let the renegade and Caleb's sister use.

Frank had, and described it. He could lead them to it with no effort. Caleb said, "We should go down right now an' brace that bastard." Ash sounded exasperated when he said, "We want to keep your sister out of it! If he's holed up an' we bust in on 'em . . . Use your head, Caleb."

"I'll sneak down there in the mornin' an' watch for him to leave," Caleb stated and this time it was George Hess who demurred. "We all go! In the mornin'! An' Frank'll do the scoutin' to make sure when Jones leaves the village. Caleb, use your gawddamned head. We got to get him while they're apart."

It was the 'apart' business that troubled Ash. He could not imagine Jones leaving Lisa behind by herself in a place where she surely could tell her story and get protection, or steal a horse and run for it.

That was uppermost in his mind when they finally struck camp in a cold predawn and went slowly down to the outskirts of the village, where their approach was noted by several barking dogs, to which they paid no attention; all villages had dogs and all dogs barked if nothing more threatening than a foraging raccoon was abroad.

They left the horses tethered in a bosque of trees after which Frank Horton led the way to the house behind the store, both of which were on the east side of town.

There was a three-sided animal shelter where they could hear a horse and inevitably someone suggested setting the renegade afoot, to which Ash pointed out that Jones would then be unable to leave the village, and the suggestion died.

The store building was the most imposing structure in Ino. It clearly did not rely upon the village for its health. There were ranches scattered throughout the vicinity. Ino, for all its drowsy appearance, was not a ghost town, not even close to being one despite its somnolent appearance.

The Nolan riders formed a loose surround, huddled from sight and blew on their fingers, waiting for the renegade to emerge, and when that ultimately happened, and Jones was an ideal target as he was briefly motionless while he took down deep breaths of the invigorating predawn air and Caleb rose to one knee with his carbine raising, a second man appeared. In poor light all the watchers could make out was that he and Jones were about the same height, but the newcomer, bundled into a rider's sheep-pelt coat, was much thicker.

They conversed briefly, something changed hands and as Jones headed for the three-sided shed the other man went to the front of the shack and leaned there with a Winchester in the crook of one arm.

Caleb held his carbine snugged for the moment Jones led his horse out to be mounted, and when that happened Ash struck Caleb's shoulder hard. Not a word passed between them as Caleb lowered the Winchester.

Jones reined northward up the alley behind the village. Ash suspected the renegade knew where he was going, was not simply riding forth as Frank Horton seemed to think, to buy fresh horses.

But Jones was no longer the objective. The man guarding the front of the shack leaned aside his Winchester to roll and light a smoke. Ash could feel Caleb tensing and jammed him in the ribs. Caleb did not relax but he flinched.

A rooster crowed, a dog barked, and a light came on in a house across from the store. Caleb growled at Ash, who responded with another sharp elbow.

The man Jones had left to make certain Lisa did not escape during his absence, removed his hat, ran bent fingers through his hair, reset the hat and leaned against the wall at his back.

George Hess appeared soundlessly to whisper to Ash after which Hess disappeared around the southerly corner of the house.

Caleb started to speak and Ash put a hand over the bearded man's mouth, held it there briefly then removed it. He and Caleb exchanged hostile stares.

A second rooster joined the first one in sounding the advent of a new day. The dog that had been barking gave it up.

Frank Horton, who had been behind the three-sided stall came stealthily to say someone was unlocking the store's roadway door. Ash nodded. If Frank had meant by innuendo for Ash to take action, it did not happen.

Ash pointed where Frank was to huddle. The three of them were near the north-east corner of the house and could smell cigarette smoke. Ash considered the streaking sky, cocked his head but heard nothing, and gradually arose to his full height. Caleb and Frank did the same. Caleb strained toward the corner of the house but Frank watched Fitzhugh.

When it happened the voice was not loud when it told the smoking guard to stand away from the wall with both arms straight out in front.

For seconds nothing happened. The guard had leaned his Winchester aside to roll the quirly, and while he had a belted six-gun it was beneath his coat.

Hess spoke again, softly. "You got one foot in the grave an' the other on a banana peel. I won't tell you again. Step clear of the house with both arms straight out."

This time the man moved and raised his arms full length. Frank Horton sighed, Ash put a restraining hand on Caleb's shoulder and led the way.

The guard heard men coming on his right side, and turned his head. Hess came from the opposite side and cocked his handgun. The guard started to swing his head, stopped moving and said, "Take her for all I care. It ain't none of my affair, but her husban' sure won't like it."

Ash kicked the door open, shoved the guard into a mouldy scented dark small parlour, and punched him roughly into a chair.

Frank lighted a hanging lamp. Caleb went charging among the rooms until he found his sister. The others could hear him asking if Jones had bothered her, and her negative muffled answer because her face was against her brother's chest in a bear hug. She said, "I begged him to let me rest. He quirted my horse and told me to keep riding."

Caleb and his sister remained in their room, Ash, Frank, George and his nephew remained in the parlour. Frank went foraging and found jerky and dry cooked spuds which he passed around, but not to the guard, who seemed more relieved than depressed at being captured. He said his name was Pete Furness, that he'd been visiting his folks but that he normally rode for the big cow outfits. He said he'd never seen Mister Jones until yesterday when Jones wanted to hire him to make sure no cowboys or other nuisances bothered his wife while he was gone. "He said there might be someone nosin' around. He paid me ten dollars, more'n I make in a week workin' cows."

Ash chewed jerky eyeing Pete Furness. Frank said, "You could have got yourself shot, mister," and the guard named Furness nodded his head without speaking. He watched Ash more than the others. When Ash said, "You got any idea where Jones went to buy horses?" Furness nodded again. "Old man Hamilton's place. He runs a few cattle but mostly deals in horses."

"Can you take us there?" Ash asked, and this time the answer was slowly and reluctantly given. "I can tell you how to get there."

George bleakly smiled and Frank Horton also did. Whatever else Pete Furness was, maybe even a top hand, he did not appear to have much stomach for getting any further involved in the trouble he was now in, if he could help it.

Randy went back for the horses, Ash, Frank and George took Furness with them to the general store, asked the big-eyed proprietor if Ino had a jailhouse and when the storekeeper said it was a steel cage across the road behind the harness works, he handed over the key and watched from the doorway as the strangers herded Pete Furness around behind the harness works, locked him in, and Ash hurled the big brass key as far as he could throw it.

In a hamlet no larger than Ino moccasin telegraph provided every inhabitant with information about the strangers in their midst, and as folks had done before, many times, Ino's residents remained out of sight. Even the dogs were taken inside and while an occasional person milked a cow or fed chickens, in general the place maintained an impression of not being inhabited.

Ash told Caleb to get a horse for his sister and start back. Caleb looked steadily at Ash and slowly shook his head.

George Hess rolled his eyes skyward. Frank and Randy lingered at the tie rack out front of the store in silence, the village around them was still and almost totally silent, except for a pair of roosters trying to out-crow each other, and dawnlight spread until an unblemished new day arrived.

Ash returned to the store and asked the proprietor for directions to the outfit run by a horse-trader named Hamilton. The storekeeper drew a map on a piece of brown wrapping-paper. Ash thanked him and returned to the roadway. Frank Horton dryly said, "I wouldn't have believed that guard either."

12

Hemp Rope and A-Horseback

THEY did not make it all the way to the Hamilton place. When they started up a wide, long and low land swale they heard a horse whinny.

They stopped on the south side where Ash sent George to scout the topout. Hess hadn't been up there more than five minutes when he came back in a breathless lope.

"He's not alone," he said out loud. "There's two riders with him, each one is leadin' a horse. Jones is ridin' between them."

Ash turned to face Caleb and Lisa. He levelled a finger at Caleb. "I'm not goin' to tell you this ever again. *You stay out of it!* Find a place where she'll be safe an' you go there an' gawddamn you, Caleb, stay there!"

There was no mistaking the fact that Ash Fitzhugh's patience with Lisa's brother was exhausted. He sat twisted in the saddle waiting for Caleb's smouldering stare to shift, and when it finally did Ash said, "Let's drift along this swale westerly. When they come around it . . . One chance to shed their guns, then we pile into them."

Randy said, "Mister Fitzhugh, them other two are maybe just leadin' the horses along as a favour."

George would have addressed his nephew but Ash beat him to it. "If they are, Randy, they'll shed their weapons. If they don't do that, we got to figure they're maybe friends of Jones."

There was warmth and perfect visibility. Except that the slope they rode easterly was matted with grass the three riders shortly to appear around the west end of the landswell could have been riding animals which would have picked up sounds.

Before they saw the riders and the

led-horses they heard someone roughly laugh. George was sitting stirrup with Ash. He softly said, "Do it again, you son of a bitch. It'll be your last."

When they came around the landswell Jones and the man on his right were gazing ahead, but the farthest rider who was leading a sorrel horse was looking at Jones — and beyond, where four mounted men sat like statues. He seemed too stunned to speak for seconds, then they saw him speak. That was when each man dismounted, swung their horses in front and levelled Winchesters across saddle seats.

Ash called out, "Shed your weapons an' turn the horses loose!"

For Randy Huffington, who would remember this moment for a very long number of years, this was the only time he would have sworn his heart stopped.

The men leading horses, all three of them, stopped stone still.

Ash called again. "Five seconds. Four seconds. Three seconds!" The man who had been leading the sorrel horse on the far side of Jones dropped the shank, spun his horse and rode back the way he had come in a belly-down run.

Ash hung fire before making the final count. He addressed the man on Jones's right side. "Two seconds, mister. You don't stand the chance of a snowball in hell."

This rider did an odd thing. He handed the shank to the horse he was leading to the renegade, muttered something and turned northward, departing at a slow walk, not a dead run.

Jones's instinctive reach for the lead shank had been with his right hand. No genuine horseman ever held their reins in the right hand.

There was not a sound and except for Jones's horse lowering its head to relieve the pressure of the reins, there was not a movement.

Ash cocked his carbine as he said, "One second!" Then more saddle guns were cocked.

Jones dropped the shank, touched the horn and swung to the ground.

Ash said, "The pistol, an' be gawddamned careful!"

Jones reached under his coat, moving slowly, lifted out the six-gun and dropped it.

Ash sent Hess to get the gun and the horse. He told the renegade to walk ahead of the horse, which Jones did.

George Hess softly frowned and looked in the direction of his nephew. He quietly said, "Boy, go back to them bushes and shed your underpants."

When Jones was close Ash eased down the dog on his carbine. The others did the same. Ash said, "Where's the money?"

"Inside my shirt. You want it?"

"No. Walk ahead of us. I'll tell you when to stop. Walk back the way you come. *Walk!*"

Jones walked. In after years the riders herding him found reason to grudgingly respect the renegade. Whatever else he was, he was not a coward.

They halted along the slope where Caleb and his sister sat their horses like wooden Indians. Ash turned to George and Frank. They both nodded without taking their eyes off Jones. Ash pointed and Caleb dismounted, stopped in front of the renegade and said, "I'm goin' to kill you with my hands."

George leaned holding a lariat rope, and jutted his jaw in the direction of a tree. Caleb looked up. His three companions nodded without speaking.

They helped Caleb get the renegade to the tree and as Caleb flung the rope over a limb the renegade said, "I'll see every one of you sons of bitches in Hell!"

Ash went back where Lisa was standing with her horse, took her firmly by the shoulders and turned her completely around. He remained with her like that until he heard George, his nephew and Frank returning with Caleb bringing up the rear, then he helped her mount and managed to stay on her blind side as they started back the way they had come.

It was not a long ride but it seemed to be. No one spoke, the sun slid off dead centre, Ino eventually hove into sight and Ash made a wide sashay around the place.

They rode until dusk then camped, shared what little they had to eat, hobbled the horses, settled down under one blanket each and did not awaken until the sun was in their eyes.

It was a long ride back. They stopped at the homesteader's place, paid him handsomely for a decent meal prepared by his wife who avoided eye contact with everyone except Lisa, and after the Nolan riders were on their way again the woman told her husband there should have been one more rider. Her husband solemnly nodded without saying a word.

There was no need to push the animals so they didn't, but it was near dusk of another day before some conversation emerged, and for the most part that had to do with some topics which were safe under any circumstances, the weather, the condition of the range, how well the horses had stood up — which actually was not very well — and what condition Mister Nolan would be in when they got back. Caleb mumbled, "Dead, I hope," and got some disapproving stares from the others, his sister included.

On their last day they emerged from the lava bed and Ash led the way to his creek and old camp. They ignored what remained of the camp, sent Lisa berry hunting, stripped down and soaked in creek water, would have also washed their clothing but they would not remain in this place long enough for them to dry, so they redressed and waited for Lisa to return. When she did she glared at Ash. "There's no berries here." She saw their wet hair and steady gazes, blushed and went to prepare a meal from what the homesteaders had put into their saddle-bags.

Lisa counted stars, measured in inches the changing course of the moon, listened to snoring men, went down to the creek and also took an all over bath, but in her case the water was colder, there was no sunshine to dry her, so she got back under her blanket and awaited first light. By then she expected to be dry. And she was. It hadn't been an entirely satisfactory bath.

The final leg of the trip was mostly uphill using the trail Ash had led them over several days before, and when they reached the plateau their horses were stumbling.

The old dog barked but only a few times. Otherwise there was no sign of life in the yard or over at the main house.

They cared for their animals, washed their backs, grained and hayed them and latched the gate, leaving the chain hanging loose.

Old man Wolff was rocking in a chair on the porch by the time they were ready to cross the yard.

He nodded as though they had only been gone a short while, but sat straight when Ash dumped the money in his lap as he asked about Mister Nolan. Lisa's father counted bills twice, and finally handed the bills to his daughter. He had learned long ago at his mammy's knee to count to one hundred, a sum she had felt certain he would never have to count in excess of, and she was right, at least until the sundown years of his life.

Ash pushed on inside, the kitchen was a mess. He passed to the gloomy passageway and stopped in the bedroom doorway where Fred Nolan also nodded as though they had last seen each other a few hours earlier. He said, "You find the son of a bitch?"

Ash nodded, tipped back his hat and sat on the bedside chair.

"Shoot him, did you?"

"Hanged him, Mister Nolan. Caleb and Lisa come back."

"No one hurt?"

"No. You been makin' out all right, have you?"

Nolan pinched his forehead into a slight frown. "Considerin' everyone deserted me, I did. Willford Wolff can't change a bandage for sour apples."

Ash leaned. "It looks all right to me. Don't show any blood."

"Where's Lisa? I'd like to see her."

As Ash arose Nolan had a question for him. "Well, what'll it be? You goin' to fish or cut bait?"

"Haven't made up my mind yet, Mister Nolan," Ash replied and went to find Lisa Wolff.

Caleb stood squarely in the barn doorway, legs spread, arms folded. When Ash asked about his sister Caleb answered in a growl. "She's out back takin' an all-over bath at the trough."

"Tell her Mister Nolan wants to see her," Ash said and started to turn away.

Caleb halted him. "Mister Fitzhugh, I'd like a word with you."

Ash turned back, irritable and weary.

"How long we known each other, Caleb?"

The bearded man's brow faintly wrinkled. "I'd say about three months or so. Why?"

"You know my first name? It is Ash."

Caleb's brow cleared. "Ash — my pa went home now that we're back. He showed me the money. I'm obliged to you. We all are. Mind a personal question?"

"Try me, Caleb."

"Are you goin' to stay? Work for Mister Nolan?"

"I don't know. Him an' I don't seem to hit it off very good."

"Ash — you'n me never hit it off good neither, but I'm here to tell you I'm goin' to work on that. Us Wolffs never forget a favour." Caleb held out a ham-sized hand.

Ash considered it, shook and dropped the hand. "Tell Lisa Mister Nolan wants to — "

"I'll do that."

"Where's the others?"

"At the bunkhouse rasslin' up a decent meal . . . Ash? Take Nolan up on it. That's how things should be up here. Friends all around."

Ash eyed the burly man. "You'n Mister Nolan?"

Caleb gave a direct answer. "He kept his word to my pa, handed over the money."

"You figure a mean son of a bitch like that's got to have some good in him?"

Caleb nodded, recrossed his arms and remained in his wide-legged stance.

Ash went to the bunkhouse. The moment he opened the door the aroma struck him. Meat and potato stew garnished with onions. The eating men at the table looked up. George Hess gestured with a large spoon in the direction of the stove and went back to eating.

The sun climbed, exhausted men and animals slept on full stomachs Over at the main house Mister Nolan told Lisa to sit. She took the bedside chair. He cleared his throat not once but twice, flicked her a look and looked at the empty doorway before beginning to speak. "There's a paper on the parlour table. Give it to your pa. It's the quit claim. I put in it the lot of you can live over there as long as you want to or need to. I'll let Caleb help me make a gate cut to replace the cattle, and he can go through my remuda for the horses."

He looked at the girl. She was sitting with both hands folded in her lap. It was hard to tell from her expression what her thoughts might be and Fred Nolan did not make the effort as he resumed speaking.

"I was goin' to put into the quit claim that you'd tend me until I can be up and around . . . but that didn't belong there, it belongs between us."

"I'll do it as long as you need me, Mister Nolan."

He looked steadily at her for a long moment before speaking again. "I'll tell you somethin' I'd never tell another livin' soul. I wish you was fifteen years older'n I was fifteen years younger."

Lisa did not speak.

"Well, I had to say that, for all it's worth, which ain't a hell of a lot."

"You'll pull through, Mister Nolan. You just got to stop gettin' out of that bed, an' even when you can, you'll have to mind what you do for a long time."

"An' who'll run things, young lady? I built this outfit up over half a lifetime."

"Ash will, Mister Nolan. Ash and the riders you hired."

"Ash never said he'd stay."

"He will. You got to work on that too. He's not the kind that takes to bullyin'."

Nolan started to redden. "Me bully a feller that big an' young?"

Lisa smiled slightly. "Treat him like you'd treat a son, Mister Nolan. Or the way you'd like to be treated."

Nolan started to lean and Lisa

pushed him back. "What do you want?"

"That jug your pa put down there somewhere."

She picked up the jug and held it while he swallowed twice, then did not allow her to take the jug away until he'd swallowed one more time. As he blew out a flammable breath he said, "I never liked whiskey. Burnt my gullet an' left a taste in my mouth like the bottom of a bird cage. But, Lisa, if I'd known your pa made anythin' like that sippin' whiskey we'd have been friends a long time ago."

"Will you talk to Ash?" she asked, and Nolan got a sly look on his face. "You do it. For some blessed reason you can get him to do things I can't."

When she left the house Ash, George Hess and Frank Horton were sitting on the small bunkhouse porch. When Ash asked about Randy his uncle jerked his head. "Caleb's showin' him how to tie a squaw hitch so's if they have to do some packin' the lad'll know how it's done." George turned and said, "Lisa's lookin' for you, Ash." George winked at Frank. Without a word they strolled in the direction of the barn. Lisa barely noticed them. She stepped under the overhang, pointed to a chair and said, "He wants you to stay, Ash. He's an old man an' he's been hurt."

"Hurt maybe, but not old. He don't act old anyway."

"He's almost as old as my pa. Ash, I know he's got a disposition like a bear with a sore behind, but honestly, since I've got to know him, he's an awful lot of bark an' a lot less bite."

"Tell that to your pa an' your brother. He ran off your cattle an' — "

"Listen to me! Maybe he'll never get plumb tame but for a fact he's got the makin's of a lot better man than I figured all these years."

He looked at her. When she was intense she was different. He said, "You want me to stay?"

"Yes!"

"An' be his rangeboss?"

"Yes!"

"Lisa . . . any other reason?"

She coloured to the hairline but did not take her eyes off his face, and she swore, something he couldn't remember ever having heard her do before.

"Yes, damn it! But you got no call to ask a question like that!"

He watched her stamp all the way over to the main house, heard her slam the door, and smiled.

He stayed. Lisa Wolff and Ashley Fitzhugh were married the following December, when there was two feet of snow on the ground, the main house was ablaze with light, old man Wolff and Fred Nolan sat by the fire sipping jug-liquor as mellow as apple cider.

There was only one solemn face. Randy had known he was too young and she was too old, but puppy-love could strike at any time. He was growing up; not many youths his age had ridden down a renegade and witnessed his hanging.

FIGHTING RAMROD
Charles N. Heckelmann

Most men would have cut their losses, but Frazer counted the bullets in his guns and said he'd soak the range in blood before he'd give up another inch of what was his.

LONE GUN
Eric Allen

Smoke Blackbird had been away too long. The Lequires had seized the Blackbird farm, forcing the Indians and settlers off, and no one seemed willing to fight! He had to fight alone.

THE THIRD RIDER
Barry Cord

Mel Rawlins wasn't going to let anything stand in his way. His father was murdered, his two brothers gone. Now Mel rode for vengeance.